Waltzing Hearts

Krish

Ukiyoto Publishing

All global publishing rights are held by

Ukiyoto Publishing

Published in 2023

Content Copyright © Krish

ISBN 9789360498061

All rights reserved.

No part of this publication may be reproduced, transmitted, or stored in a retrieval system, in any form by any means, electronic, mechanical, photocopying, recording or otherwise, without the prior permission of the publisher.

The moral rights of the author have been asserted.

This is a work of fiction. Names, characters, businesses, places, events, locales, and incidents are either the products of the author's imagination or used in a fictitious manner. Any resemblance to actual persons, living or dead, or actual events is purely coincidental.

This book is sold subject to the condition that it shall not by way of trade or otherwise, be lent, resold, hired out or otherwise circulated, without the publisher's prior consent, in any form of binding or cover other than that in which it is published.

www.ukiyoto.com

Dedication

The book Waltzing Hearts was made possible by the enthusiasm and constant support of my family. I am indebted to my mother Swapna and my father Rabindra for their care and understanding in nurturing me up. I would like to thank my four sisters Sarmista, Sharmila, Sushree, and Sonali, who proved instrumental in writing this book. I dedicate this book to the readers for whom this story was penned down. Lastly my warm gratitude to Ukiyoto Publishing and their supportive team who showed faith in my work and helped me published it.

Contents

Nightfall	1
Sparkling Mist	6
Smiles and Roses	12
Little Angels	16
Guiding Music	19
A Parting Gift	24
Nightingale's Melody	26
Falling in Love	35
Martini Effect	43
Frozen Falls	55
The Rider	57
Two Lives	60
Pandemonium	62
Awakening	64
Farewell	68
Nostalgia	75
Entangled Feelings	78
Friends' Day Out	85
Beer Fest	89
The Reaper's Wrath	97
Heart Strings	106
Prelude To Winter	109
A Piper's Kiss	118
Polaris	134
Vows	150
March 29	157
The Tilted Promise	165
Faulted Lines	175

A New Life	177
A Summer Meeting	181
Season of Fall	185
Winter Frost	190
A Dead End	193
Heartbeats	194
Interlude	201
Memories Rekindled	206
Phoenix Soul	210
Epilogue	213
About the Author	***Error! Bookmark not defined.***

Nightfall

It was winter of 2009. Shaira lay covered in snow. Everything was still. So silent and peaceful. It was the perfect place. For loneliness seemed plentiful joyous to me. And this place respected one's privacy. That's why I chose to move here.

With heavy snow outdoors, most of my time was spent idly. I had no computer, nor cell phone, nor TV. I lived a simple life. That seemed enough.

Today was no different. I lay on the sofa reading Sherlock Holmes. He intrigued me as he did to everybody. Deductions, methodological stuff, he was pretty good.

The clock struck past nine. It was time for dinner. Well, a bit of bread, butter and a glass of milk. That sufficed me. As I started ascending the steps, a knock resounded on the door. I thought it was the wind. But it struck again.

Lazily with the elegant pace of a turtle, I walked towards the square piece of wood. I unlocked the hinge and had just opened it when a cold shivery wind blew past my face.

In front of me stood a figure like a snowman cladded in a coat with its cheeks barely visible. Eyes darting out in search of response.

"Come inside please," I told the visitor.

Without answering, it budged past me, straight to the bonfire in front, and warmed itself. I closed the door behind and pondered about the identity of this untimely visitor.

A few minutes passed completely silent before the visitor spoke.

"Than.......nk you," it said. That was the voice of a female I pondered. It sounded a bit American with an English style.

She took her coat off and placed it on the sofa nearby. As she did so, I observed the following

Slim body, fairly tall, white coloured with a tattoo of Auroborus on her left hand. A brunette with a ponytail hanging behind her turtle collared black shirt. Black, fairly expensive snow boots. Denim jeans and a ring on her first right finger.

As she turned towards me, I saw her face. "Pretty" that be apt to describe her. But it puzzled me, it strung a chord in my memory and I didn't know why.

Still warming herself near the fire she spoke.

"I am a journalist,"

"And you're here to film the Juancos," I deduced.

"Yes..."

Juancos are unknown birds that fly here during winter. Strange as it sounds, they nest here for a month before flying away someplace else that nobody ever knows.

"But my car broke down and I had to walk a fair distance before I found this house,"

"Your cameraman?" I asked curious.

"Men slow you down that's what I believe..."

That seemed crude but true.

"Hence I came alone,"

I knew from there on that she's a feisty lady to argue with.

"Okay then..." I said walking to the refrigerator and looking for something called food. I had five loaves of bread, half a dozen eggs. Add a bit of onion, some oil and omelette's ready. That'd be enough I thought.

I placed the necessary items on the table and said with a gasp, "Here's your food."

She looked a bit puzzled. But I continued talking anyway.

"I'm going upstairs to sleep. You can eat the omelette and sleep on the sofa,"

"But I don't know cooking..." she said while I was walking up the staircase.

"And neither do I. Besides you'll manage, I'd only slow you down, won't I?" I said before slamming the door shut and leaving her swearing, "Askhole"

And so here, I found myself lying on my bed as I waited to hear some noise. Five minutes passed, then another five, and ultimately after half an hour I ran out of patience. I opened the door only to find that the eateries were lying cold on the table and the girl had fallen asleep.

I alighted down, walked towards the kitchen and began making the omelette.

Add a bit of oil, then crack the egg into two, stir it well in the frying pan. Some salt to chisel it up with onions cut into thin slices. Warm the bread a bit and serve it hot.

I dragged a small table in front of the sofa and put the plate there. Job's done. But the girl was still asleep.

She must have been really tired. But I had to wake her up and it took quite an effort.

I nudged her by her shoulders, tried calling her, and ultimately took the final step. Pour some water on the sleeping beauty's face. As I did so, she awoke surprised and swearing.

"You a....why did you do that?" she shouted. I turned away and walked up stairs with the final words of the night,

"Eat it or else you'll catch a cold. There's a blanket by your side. It'll help if you need it."

Finally, I lay on my bed. Let's sleep.

"There was a cry, full of terror. People had gathered around. I saw and heard frantic voices as it rained and I kept running recklessly. A car might have knocked me down but I got up and kept running. I arrived at last.

As I made my way through, I saw a blood-stained knife lying on the road. Alas! I was too late..."

I awoke with a gasp trying to calm down. But I couldn't. I just couldn't let go of them. Their memories kept haunting me. Neither time nor distance eased the guilt. No matter how I saw it, it always deepened the wound.

Getting off bed, I walked downstairs to check on my unexpected visitor. The plate was empty, she was asleep and Luce, my pet dog and only companion was lying next to the sofa.

As she saw me, her tail started wagging and she sprung on to me. It's a gesture meaning she was hungry. Hence, I got her bowl and poured over some biscuits before laying it on the floor. She gulped down those bits instantly and barked. It meant I'm still hungry.

That bark awoke the sleeping lady and she stood on her sofa surprised and screaming

"Holy bejesus...That...dog...is it yours?" she stuttered.

"Yes,"

"...Uh...I didn't notice it last night...Does it bite?"

"First of all, it's a she and she does bite,"

"Bites," she exclaimed.

"Yes, but only at those who act like a buffoon,"

"Very funny..." she said sardonically still staring at the dog.

Luce meanwhile had finished her bowl. She took a glance at her and pranced towards the sofa.

The lady started jumping and bickering while Luce climbed on and started licking her hands. At first she screamed but she gradually realized Luce was friendly.

And so reluctance gave way to friendship, and certainly afraid but not scared she inched her hands over Luce's head and for the first time patted a dog.

"See she likes you," I said.

"Yeah...and thank you for last night," she replied politely.

"Don't bother,"

"Well it's rare for a man to help a stranger,"

"Nope. You're no stranger. Your name's Lisa Sparks. You work for Times. And you're feisty"

"How'd you know...?"

"The name's written on your bag with the channel's logo. And previous night, I guess, justifies my last remark,"

Lisa was a bit ashamed but nonetheless she was brave enough to apologize.

"Sorry for calling you a-hole. I was frustrated and angry,"

"Never mind. So do you want something to eat?" I said with a smile.

And thus the incident got shrugged off.

Sparkling Mist

Well he's a stranger. Yet he's the kindest person I've met so far. You'll think he's boring. But very often the persons who are most reserved are the most interesting ones.

Yeah I wish to see him again, but we are far apart. Too far apart that we don't talk anymore.

I miss Shaira. Such an intoxicating place and Christoff so loving and helpful.

Six years that's the time we've been apart. I came to that place looking to capture moments of a lifetime instead I lost my heart there. Such a fool nah.

Well the first morning I spent with him has been etched into my memory. The storm outside had stopped. Skies were clear and the cold not so stinging. As I sat with Luce beside me, he emerged from the kitchen holding a platter.

"Here's your breakfast," he said putting the dish on the glass.

As I picked the cover off, a delightful scent of coffee sprinkled with cream and an aroma of fresh cooked Lawquiti sandwich seared into my memory.

I took a dig in. And it was sumptuous. While I enjoyed my food, Christoff ate an apple as he stared outside the window.

"Thank you. You cook well," I said heartily.

"Glad you liked it," he replied.

As I sat there eating I observed the simple home in which Christoff lived. Well to say it was a quiet place, full of tranquillity wasn't fair. But in bare terms it was intriguing. No TV, no modern tech save the cooking ones. It's as if that guy wanted to shield himself away from the outside world.

"So Miss Sparks, how do you intend to film those creatures?" he interrupted into my thoughts with a mystical smile.

"Well, there's my equipment, you see. And I've got this tiny little button camera. That should do me well,"

"Ok…But a piece of advice. Don't go to the Shaira Lake at night,"

"May I know why?" I asked curious.

"Because it gets very dangerous out there, particularly in this winter,"

"Uh hum…I see you're trying to scare me," I said challenged.

"Nah…You ain't the type that gets scared. You're just too naïve to understand what I just said,"

And so time passed and soon that moment came.

It was nine and I had to get going. I took my coat and my equipment kit and walked towards the door.

Christoff however stood motionless at the window.

Thinking it be rude I took a card from my coat pocket and called out to him.

"Mr. Myers, thank you for everything. If you need my help be sure to call me," I said handing over my card.

"Yeah sure," he said.

And so I walked out to film the Juancos.

Snow covered the paths and treading was a bit difficult. But as I walked on, I discovered the locality there. People though not rich here, had the basics of living. Above all they were hospitable enough to clear the roads of snow for visitors.

Not knowing when I'd reach Shaira Lake, the journey proved tiresome. Occasionally I'd sit on some stranger's doorstep and catch my breath.

I had called my assistant uphill to tow my car out of the snow. Carefree and confident to film those birds I marched on.

However, there was bit of a problem. I reached at crossroads and was unsure whether to go straight or take a left. My mobile map didn't help me at all.

While I stood pondering, something hit my shoulder. As I turned round I saw a football lying on the road. A little boy, probably 11 years old, was running for it. He was alone and was playing on the cleared up grass beside the road.

"Sorry sister," he chubbled.

"It's okay kid,"

He picked up the ball and started dribbling all the while playing alone.

I looked about and saw an orphanage named "Teresa". A nun was standing at the door and watching over all the kids who played in front.

I walked over to her in search of help.

"Sister I'm lost here a bit,"

"Lost. No one's lost until you give up hope," she said with serenity.

"Yeah that's true. Can you tell me the way to Shaira Lake?"

"The lake....Yes, take a right here and then keep walking straight until you reach a turnabout. Take a left and you're there,"

"Thank you,"

"You're welcome child,"

With that remark I turned to leave but my curiosity got the better of me and I couldn't help asking

"Sister why's the boy playing alone there?"

"Oh that's August. He lives with his mother in the opposite house. I guess he's a bit shy,"

"Shy…huh," I replied before walking off again.

Treading along at last I saw a glimpse of the lake. It was frozen over. Yet life had found its way below this icicle. The shivery blades of grasses, the fluttering of strange petals, and the monotony and tranquillity of this place was lying beckoning for spring to waltz into their lives.

The sight was a spectacle that I had to capture. And no sooner, my camera was in my hands synchronously clicking images.

The Juancos had only been reported at night. So I camped there waiting for dusk to fall over. I at times got impatient but had my iPod to soothe me. For food I had a couple of burritos which were given by Christoff should I need it.

Slowly and surely dusk fell over and the melody of these unpictured birds raptured the lakeside. With tippy-toe feet I placed my camera holder behind a hedge nearby and squatted on my thighs in anticipation.

It seemed eternity but finally an illuminating blue tail outlined by black flashes emerged behind a tree. I calmed my excitement down but failed as my heartbeat was too fast. Just a little bit more I urged the bird in my mind. Then suddenly a lightning struck in the lake. An ear deafening thunder followed it. The vicinity got covered into dense mist blocking my vision.

"Crap," I said cursing my luck.

Then something extraordinarily followed. The sound of a lullaby as if from a piano harmonized into my ear, I saw the outline of a huge bird emerging out of the mist before spreading its enormous wings against the moonlit sky, my eyes became weary until I sensed out falling asleep onto the grass.

Rays of morning sun glistened onto my cold body as I lay motionless on the wet grass. My ears, hands and legs were numb. My face had frost bite and it ached. The morning sky seemed so serene yet that wasn't my main concern.

"What could have sparkled that iridescent blinding blue light?" I pondered.

My camera holder was still in place but I doubt it could have captured anything. As I lay pondering, the outline of a human could be seen running towards me before I blacked out again.

Was I dead? No I'm dreaming. It has to be.

Those were the notions I underwent when I first opened my eyes. However I found myself lying on a bed with a blanket over me. Beside me there sat a boy familiar to my memory.

As he noticed I was awake, he ran out of the room and probably descended down a flight of stairs screaming "Mother! Mother! She's awake. The lady's awake,"

"Easy there August. I'm coming up to see her," said a gentle feminine voice.

A fair lady, probably in her thirty's, entered into the room. She was a brunette, and had a charming sweet voice.

"How are you feeling?" she asked tenderly.

"....Fine," I tried my best to speak.

"It's okay. The cold has subdued your voice. Take some rest now."

I nodded my head after which she walked out of the room.

Alone and sick the only thing I could do was to look. I lay in a small but well-to-do room. Simple and cosy would suffice to describe the decorations and utility. However there was this picture that caught my eye.

In front of the bed against a red wall there stood a picture of this lady, and his husband. She had a bulge in her stomach and they looked like a really happy couple. As I kept scrutinizing the room, an hour had passed by, before she entered opening the door.

She was holding a plate in her hand. Putting it beside a low table by the bedside she sat beside me.

"Here have some of this," she said holding a bowl out to me.

I huddled up on my back to the bedside and ate the soup she offered to me.

While drinking the soup many questions were plundering my empty brain. However my body needed the food more than it needed the answer as to "How I got here?"

"Lie down. And get some rest," she said and began to leave.

"Wait," I said.

"Yes. Do you need something?" she asked caringly.

"What's your name?"

"It's Trisha,"

"Thank you for saving my life there,"

"O! It's not me who got you here. It was Christoff,"

"Christoff?"

"Yes. He saw you lying there out in the cold when he went to that lake to collect some herbs for me,"

"Herbs?"

"Yes I'm somewhat of a doctor,"

"....Still then thank you,"

"You're welcome," she took leave as the day passed with Trisha taking care of me.

Smiles and Roses

"**V**ery often we fear things that we don't know. Consequences, ifs, and shoulds they all jumble up ultimately crippling us to dare. But it's better to have said those words and gotten rejected than forever spending your life in uncertainty,"

"Such philosophy is junk," he commented.

"Well it's true," I replied sharply.

"True? Well then hear me out. Here's a kid who admires his neighbour next door. He doesn't know what love is. He's simply fascinated by her beauty,"

"What does that mean?"

"It means he's attracted towards her but his shyness troubles him. I don't wanna lecture him your trash philosophy, I just want to give him a chance,"

"Chance to do what?" I said sardonically

"To be friends with her,"

"You think he's gonna speak a word in front of her,"

"Nope. He doesn't need to,"

"Alright this is getting irritating. Tell me what you're gonna do,"

"Just wait and watch," he said with a smile.

Leaving me curious Christoff walked away and I wondered how this conversation had started.

Earlier this morning I was lying on my bed when he tapped at the door. He entered in with a casual smile holding a bouquet of roses. Not red ones. But ice blue ones. Their colour was strange but then again what I saw the night before yesterday was even stranger.

He placed it in a vase by the bedside and talked very calmly.

"Your equipment bag is downstairs, okay," he said

"Thank you,"

"Well... I have a free advice for you then,"

"What?"

"Don't film those birds secretly,"

"Why not?" I said curious.

"Because...."

His statement was interrupted by Miss Trisha's arrival.

"It's so nice of you to come here," she said to him.

"Yes this house feels warm you know," he said.

"Warm indeed if love resides," she said glancing at me.

Hold it. She thinks me and him. That's gross.

"No...You got it wrong," I said while getting up.

"Yeah, terribly wrong" Christoff supported.

"I do. Then why the Humming Roses" she asked with a smile.

"Humming Roses," I said confused.

"Yes, these ones only grow once in four years that too when the Juancos hum their sleeping melody,"

"Sleeping?"

"Okay, I better leave" said Christoff

"Well not so much of hurry," Trisha said holding his hand.

"You must help her," she said with a command in her voice.

"That ain't my business," he replied back.

"Well she can't alone film them without assistance,"

I barged into their conversation and said, "I don't need his help,"

Suddenly a temper appeared on Miss Trisha's elegant composure.

"Okay... both of you get downstairs and wait," she said commandingly.

Her audacity compared to her calmness really startled us both and we replied in unison.

"Yes Mam."

"Better," she confirmed.

While we sat downstairs Trisha got into her kitchen preparing something.

We two sat on the opposite ends of the sofa but were staring outside the same window. August was once again playing all alone and occasionally glancing at that girl.

"Well that's truly sad," I uttered subconsciously.

"What's sad?" he asked.

"Trisha's son. He likes that girl over there but is really shy,"

"Wait August likes Eve. That's gonna take some time to sink in,"

"Her name's Eve then. How do you know?"

"I often visit that place,"

"Wish I could help him,"

"But wishing doesn't change reality,"

"Okay what do you suggest?"

"Nothing. I don't mingle in child stuff,"

"You're useless,"

"Well what does sleeping prancing blockhead suggest?"

"How dare you address me like that you jack---"

"Okay I'm sorry, but did you realize what just happened?"

"Well what happened?"

"I incited you and you reacted. Newton's law. It's applicable in the real world."

For a moment I really thought who this Christoff actually was. He was insensitive, a complete jack, and yet a very insightful and helping person.

"That's it. I got it. Let's give him some advice," I said with renewed vigour while a bulb lit up in my head.

"What advice?" He said confused.

And that's how smiles and roses got confided in the first place.

Little Angels

"Hey there, can I play with you,"

"....Sure,"

He took the ball and kicked it towards me.

I tried to dribble a bit and out it went between his legs. He nevertheless kept chasing while I kept possession.

"I see you're a good kid. But why do you play alone?" I said dribbling.

"I can't make friends,"

"Make friends? That's easy,"

"Sounds easy,"

"Okay I'll teach you then,"

"Teach, but what?"

"Teach you how to talk to that girl," I said stopping the ball.

As he saw the direction of my gaze, his cheeks turned a bit red.

"You like her?" I asked.

"......Yes," he said reluctantly.

Before we could proceed further a voice entered my ear, and I turned to see Trisha calling.

"Come here. Breakfast's ready," she said to him.

He took the ball with him and left running probably too shy.

I began to leave but for her words

"You too Christoff," she said.

"No I think I'll pass," I replied and left.

As I walked through this cold weather, memories rekindled in front of my eyes.

I was a baby when someone left me at the doorsteps of an orphanage. There the sisters found me lying in a basket wrapped in red. They took me in as their own, named me and sooner than I knew I was a family member of "Little Angels" as my beloved Grandma called us. I spent my childhood in the company of my friends. But every now and then the question arose in my mind "Why did they leave me?" and the answer never came.

This recollection made me miss Grandma. She was living only two blocks from where I was, so I decided to pay a visit.

"Here let's say our prayers before we eat," said Mrs. Trisha.

"Where did Christoff go?" I asked.

"He left," she said and we started praying. The breakfast was sumptuous and I was famished. So I ate heartily. Occasionally Trisha would talk about Shaira and its people but my attention was always directed towards that guy.

"So how do you know Christoff?" I asked curious.

"Well, he's a friend of my husband. When we moved to Shaira 2 years back, he helped us settle in. As much as I know him, he's a humble person. Helpful as well,"

"He doesn't match your description though," I chuckled

"No... He's always like that. He appears cold outside but is a nice person,"

"So what does he know about these birds?"

"Well he's the only person to have seen them,"

"Wait.... many reporters come here, and even one of them wrote an article about them. Yeah what's the name?"

"C. Joel," she helped me out.

"Yeah that's right,"

"Well that is the pseudonym under which Christoff wrote the article,"

"He wrote it," I said surprised.

"You see many reporters did come here, but everybody ended up like you did. They fell asleep no matter what they did. Some even tried to place the camera there for a night, but when they returned the next morning their cameras didn't work,"

"That's creepy,"

"So it sounds."

We had finished our breakfast after which I checked my camera. The result was the same. It was all white.

"Curse it," I said.

"Told you so," said Trisha.

"Okay do you have his number?"

"He doesn't have one. I once visited his home. He lives without any modern equipment save the cooking ones,"

"He's truly....."

"Strange right. A guy like him, no family, no associates. Wonder why he chooses to live like that,"

"Yeah."

I had seven days left. And any attempt to film those birds would prove futile, that I knew. My only hope, thus was to convince that Myers to help me. Walking back would take 3 hours, so as soon as I finished eating I began to leave.

"Good luck filming those birds," said Trisha as I bade them goodbye.

I trudged along perpetually. My assistant would have gotten the car out, but I couldn't risk being stuck any further for the car tires were not made for snow. So I had instructed him to stay at lodgings uphill.

"Finally," I exclaimed with exhaustion when I reached the familiar house.

I walked up the little flight of steps onto the wooden porch and knocked at the door. There was no reply. This continued for some time after which I realized he wasn't home. I walked about here and there until I took a seat at the wooden low bench by the window sill.

There I waited and waited more till sleep fell over me.

Guiding Music

A hand poked at my shoulder and I started with a yell
"Ahh...." I screamed.
"Jeese, you're noisy," said Christoff.
"O! It's you I thought it to be a snowman,"
"Whatever. Tell me why you are sitting outside,"
"Uh... I came here and found the door was locked,"
"That I can deduce. I mean, why are you here?" he said while entering the key into the lock.
"Nothing specific," I said foolishly.
"Okay," the door clicked open "Just come inside first."
We entered in and I hushed to the fireplace and sat down.
As I sat on the sofa Luce came running in and jumped up, till we both lay tumbled upon the sofa. There she sat upon me licking my face.
"Pretty good for someone who's afraid of dogs," he said.
"Yeah...I'm still afraid of them but not this one,"
He went upstairs and then alighted down in his casual clothes.
"Trisha sent you here, I suppose," he said.
"Yes,"
"I can't help you..."
"....But why not?"
"Listen first!" he said "I can't help you to film them. But I can certainly help you see them,"
"I don't understand,"
"Those creatures they somehow know when you try to capture them on camera. Even if you take a pen camera, they'd still know,"

"Well if so, how did you see them?"

"Just by luck,"

"Can't you be more specific,"

"Okay... I was driving at night on the deserted road by the lakeside when something suddenly radiant sprang forth in front of the car. Surprised and shaken I pulled the brakes with all my might. Then when I went out to the front, I saw the most splendid thing that I had ever seen,"

"It was a blue, medium sized bird that glowed with radiance. Its beak was short and black. The tail was covered in excellent blue and black shadows, just like its body. Its eyes were closed and one of its wings had a cut, a deep one. Seeing that I took out the first aid box from the car's hatchback and wrapped its wounds. It lay still but was breathing. Then I held it in my arms and walked to the lakeside,"

"It was then the most marvellous thing occurred. A thunder struck in the middle of the frozen lake. Sparkling mist surrounded me. A lovely voice started in the vicinity, and was then followed by numerous similar ones. Suddenly my body started glowing as the bird in my hands started singing as well. And then I saw a huge bird shaped figure arising into the middle of the sky spreading its wings. I went closer to the lake and saw the most unscientific inexplicable thing,"

He paused for a minute and then asked me a simple question, "Do you know what a bird's egg requires to hatch?"

"Warmth," I replied

"Yes but not the Juancos. It's just the opposite and even more. You see when I advanced forward I saw hundreds of radiant blue birds all flying synchronously forming a giant figure of one bird. They were all coming out from the hole in the frozen lake. Finally its tail had emerged out and then the birds disintegrated and flew off at separate angles down to the various sides of the dense forest that surrounded me. However there was one bird that flew straight into my open palms and started caressing the injured bird with its beak. By that time the mist had cleared and everywhere, I saw small glowing blue light darting out and illuminating the moonless sky,"

"The spectacle left me spellbound. The two birds now flew out of my hands and I saw myriad Juancos flying away someplace that mankind didn't know."

His narrative had stopped. And I was left dumbfounded. What he was saying couldn't actually be possible but then again I witnessed a part of it last night.

"One thing, why did your body start glowing?" I asked

"I don't know," he said honestly, "But that night when I was about to leave I saw something glowing that lay on the ground. It was evidently the injured bird's feather. Then I picked it up as a remembrance of that fantastic night and left,"

"Do you still have it?"

"Yes,"

"Where is it?" I said with excitement.

"Upstairs,"

"Can I see it," I said like a child.

We both went up and then from one of his drawers he picked a box and gave it to me. I opened it and there it lay. Shining blue like the sea does when the sun shines the brightest.

"Goodness me," I said, "How is all of this possible?"

"I pondered that myself and came up with a few possible answers."

As I sat on the dining table, Christoff prepared some delicacy. I waited as patiently as I could but damn I was excited and couldn't help but walk straight into the kitchen.

There I saw him making a cake of chocolate. I think he noticed me but carried on with his work meticulously.

"Is it your birthday?" I asked.

"Nope,"

"Is it for a friend?"

"Yes,"

"A girlfriend, I suppose," I started teasing him.

"Sort of,"

"What's her name?"

"None of your business,"

"Does Trisha know that?"

"No,"

"Secret admirer. That's interesting,"

"Alright. Stop your pervert thinking and give me that sprinkler."

He placed the cake in the oven and then we both sat down at dining table.

"Okay here's what I can explain," he said.

"The birds glow because of bio-luminescence. Now about them coming out of ice. According to physics water's frozen up in a lake but underneath it's still liquid water. They lay their eggs sometime in the year, and leave. Now Shaira Lake is the perfect place cause lightning always strikes there in winter for some static build-up. That creates the hole. I assume and I reiterate I assume that these eggs hatch only when lightning strikes. Thus the only part left to explain is,"

"The sleeping melody, the large bird figure and above all why they need coldness to hatch,"

"Right. Now when the young bird touched my palm, it was extremely hot. So if they have abnormally high temperatures when young then that explains why cold water is needed,"

"High heat absorbing capacity without showing temperature rise," I said.

"Exactly that regulates the bird's temperature. Now that music I think orchestrates them into that formation so that they can take off at varying angles towards their mother or father which I don't know. Assuming every bird has specific voice quality which their young ones can recognize, that helps them to find their babies I guess,"

"But why didn't you fall asleep?"

"See when I touched the feather after they had left, my body didn't glow. It glowed only when I was holding the bird and when it sang,"

"You mean you were immune to sleeping,"

"I guess so,"

"Alright that's enough. That's one heck of a hypothesis but I guess it's the only one that's possible,"

"And probable,"

A beep sound echoed the room and Christoff took leave saying "Voila, it's ready."

While I sat alone I realized why nobody had ever filmed those birds and why no one could ever do so. The lightning and the mist at such a close range disables every video catching equipment. And then the rapturous melody lulls you to sleep while a fairy-tale blossoms right in front.

A Parting Gift

"You got to move past him, Lisa," said Ann sounding concerned.

"Yeah I know, but I think I'll forget about him in time," I replied.

"6 years is a long time,"

I didn't have an answer for that.

"I think you should start dating again," she pressed me.

That thought had crossed my mind before but wherever and with whoever I was, his face always invaded my mind.

"Nah. It doesn't help"

Saying that, I broke off from the conversation and walked towards the open door and then left the party in my car leaving my friend worried.

"Christoff Myers," I would love to see that person again. But I don't know if I ever could.

My life had prospered ever since I met him. I was now the editor of The Times, I owned a good sized house, and was comfortably off. However I was lonely amidst this bustling life of the city.

Life seemed to pass and my hope of seeing him was dying. But that's when fate came knocking at my door.

It was spring time. Work was few and I mostly kept indoors. Day had passed and night enshrouded my home. I started off for my room but a knock on the door halted me.

Opening the door I found a boy standing still.

"Yes may I help you," I said.

"You don't recognize me," he spoke with a smile but his eyes seemed sorrowful.

"Nope,"

"Well 6 years is a long time,"

The moment he uttered those words, my mind started to find resemblance with that face.

"August!"

"Yes,"

My reaction was one of delight and hope.

"Come in. Take a seat," I said ecstatically.

As he sat there on the settee, I prepared him some coffee.

"Here have some," said I.

"Thank you,"

"You know I have many questions to ask you. But first, I'm really glad to see you,"

"Same here,"

"So how's everyone?"

His face had turned sad. Silence ensued till sometime when he spoke at last with a heavy voice.

"Well I have come here because she asked me to. Here take this,"

He handed me a diary, and a gift wrapped in red that he took out from his pockets.

"The funeral happened a month ago. But on her death bed, she asked me to deliver this to you. She said and I quote, "Tell her to read this. The rest I'll leave up to her.""

A shock shattered my good spirits. And what followed next changed my entire life.

Nightingale's Melody

Evening had fallen and seethed itself into Shaira. Slowly stars were peeping out illuminating the streets with their joyful dance. Amidst this charmed vicinity I sat amazed at his house.

We had talked throughout the afternoon, and he had agreed to help me. So right now we were seated near the fireplace. He was sitting to my opposite in his rocking armchair, while Luce and I were seated in the sofa.

"Well it will take three days," he said.

"I can wait. Besides I would love to tour this place," I replied.

"Well that's Shaira's charm. It attracts everybody,"

The conversation drifted into many corners and subtly came the topic of love.

"So you love this person?" I asked.

"Yes. She's everything to me,"

"Everything huh. So what's her name?" I asked curiously.

"Mary,"

"Mary. Then the cake's for her. It's her birthday tomorrow I guess,"

"Yes. You can join in if you want to," he said teasing me.

"No, I'll stay here. Don't wanna hinder her special day,"

"Trust me. She'll be delighted to see someone new,"

"You're sure about that,"

"Yeah,"

"Fine, if you insist, I'll accompany you," I said without any excitement.

We dined for the night after which he went upstairs to sleep. Luce and I were now left alone in the room. I slipped onto the sofa with Luce sleeping on a small basket bed on the hearth-rug beside me. Before I went to sleep one thing came to mind, "Mary huh. She's really lucky."

First rays of the morning sun touched down my face through the open window. Christoff was in the kitchen and was carefully packing the cake.

"Good morning," I said.

"Same here. Better get ready. We'll be going in an hour."

He hurriedly went upstairs, and came down with a small gift in his hand.

After all the essentials were in, we started off the house and yes Luce came with us.

We walked quite some distance, before stopping in front of a large house.

He knocked at the door, and when it was opened, I gave a stare of embarrassment and surprise both at the same time.

In front of me stood an old lady, some sixty years old, looking at me with a smile.

"Ah I see you have brought a friend," she told Christoff in her loving manner.

"Yes, and happy birthday Grandma," he said hugging her.

"Thank you," she said and we both entered into this beautiful place of hers.

I admit Christoff was right earlier in calling me a pervert. I forgot that love is of many kinds. That was my first moment of embarrassment amidst the extraordinary feelings I was about to experience.

Grandma Mary's house was very akin to that of Christoff's. However she kept it more pristine and aesthetic than him. Well that was expected of women. Men are clumsy regarding such matters. While I was pondering these things, I heard Christoff calling me.

"Do you mind lighting it?" he asked as he placed the cake in the centre of a glass table and inserted a candle on top.

"Nope. It'd be my pleasure," I said as I struck a matchstick.

Lights were blurted out and in the centre of the room there stood the four of us. The Happy Birthday Song was recited and to add to that Luce also barked some mysterious language. I suppose it was more for the cake than to wish her.

Grandma took a slice of cake, and first gave it to me.

It surprised me a bit. She'd hardly known me, yet she was so friendly to me.

As she gave it to me she made a hilarious remark, "You know Christopher, lady's first,"

"Yeah Grandma," he replied in same spirit.

Christoff meanwhile had taken a small gift out of his pocket and handed it down to her.

She gave a motherly smile and said, "What's in this?"

"It's something I received," he said.

As she unwrapped the gift, a nostalgia fell over her face and she said, "Where'd you find it?"

"Jeffrey, found it in our old place. I'd thought it was lost during your arrival here."

The gift was a pair of old glasses but it held importance to her.

Meanwhile Luce gave a bark.

"We haven't forgotten you Luce, here you go," Grandma said as she placed a piece of cake on a plate and placed in on the linoleum.

"You haven't made breakfast, I guess," said Christoff.

"No. I won't do that. It's the only day in the year I get to eat the food you cook," she said affably.

"Well you both can sit here, I'll go and prepare something. I'll show you Grandma, my culinary skills have improved" he said and went into the kitchen.

There were twin sofa's facing opposite each other. I took a seat and so did she.

We sat silent for a minute before she spoke.

"You live in Riviera," she said.

"Yes, how did you know?"

"Your ring has a label on it,"

That comment puzzled me. Even without her glasses on she had a good eyesight.

However she clarified herself, "You see these glasses are my husband's. He died some 30 years ago, and I preserved it with me during that time. However during our arrival here, it got lost,"

"I'm sorry,"

"It's not your fault. He had cancer, and the fight eventually got the better of him,"

I had no reply to that.

"So Lisa what do you do?" she asked changing the subject.

"Well I'm a reporter,"

"Trying to film the Juancos, then,"

"Yes and sadly failing,"

"Ah that happens. I'm sure Christopher would help you,"

"Yes, he said he would,"

"So did you tour Shaira?"

"No, but I hope to during these three days,"

"I'm sure you'll find it a beautiful place. Its serene, calm and neighbours are very friendly,"

"Yes that's true,"

Grandma then looked into the kitchen and then faced towards me.

"You know I'm worried about my little kid here,"

"Christoff, but why, he seems a happy fellow,"

"Yes that's the problem. He never shows it in front of me, but I know the pain he carries,"

"Pain?"

"Yes, he blames himself for everything that happened in the past,"

Before we could chat further, Christoff entered the room with the food tray.

We sat at the table, and after our prayer, began to eat.

I had eaten the food he had cooked earlier, but this was something else.

"You certainly have improved, Christopher," she told him.

"Yeah, it tastes much better than earlier," I joined in too.

"Well let's skip the formalities, and eat," he replied.

Luce also joined in, and as a whole it felt exquisite to sit around with friends and have a quiet breakfast.

"So this is what family is about?" I thought and reminisced about mom and dad.

My dad was the typical workaholic type while mother was a free soul. She lived life on her own terms, unbounded and care-free from all obligations. Altogether I never saw them sharing light talks, nor did they ever opened up to each other.

Except the fact that they took pains in bringing me up, I owe them no other gratitude. You see, we are an estranged family. I seldom think about them, and they rarely call me save my own birthday.

But today for some reason I missed them more. May be it's just a passing thought or an ignored feeling. Anyhow I shrugged that prick off my mind and enjoyed the company of my friends.

By now we had had our breakfast and were resting, when a fateful musical hour beckoned to us. A piano was placed at the corner of the room, and Grandma insisted on me playing it.

"Sorry I have just started learning piano. I'm not good at it," I told her.

"Never mind, trying is much better than not attempting something because of fear. Besides Christopher will help you out when needed."

After much coaxing, I sat on the long bench and tried to deduce the rhythm, after which I played the tune. Initially I did good, but then I started to falter.

Just as I was about to give up, Christoff's finger got interlocked with mine and I could feel his warm breath on my cold face. My heart started beating faster and my cheeks turned red. He directed my movements effortlessly, and out of utter discord I was now playing a rapturous melody. He leaned forward against my shoulders and whispered into my ears, "Don't think here, feel the music. Everything will be fine."

Those words were of confidence. I had begun to catch the movements, and gradually Christoff pulled back and I was now playing the most serene, enchanting music I had ever heard in my life.

While I was playing, the sound of violin joined in as well. I saw Christoff playing it completely engrossed but with his thoughtful eyes towards me. Our gazes were locked for some time and a smile was on both of our faces. We were complimenting each other in tandem. So perfect was the pair, that when we finished Grandma got up and applauded.

"You two make a lovely couple," she said with a smile.

As if that was not embarrassing enough, Luce too joined in with a few barks.

We both shrugged those words off in unison, "No, you've got it wrong,"

So comical was our reply, Grandma gave a hearty laugh and said, "Come here, you two,"

We took a seat beside her and she spoke, "You know. This tune you played is the Nightingale's melody. It's difficult to get it right the first time. But you played it flawlessly,"

"That doesn't mean we are a couple," we said again in unison

"No. You're not. But neither was your Grandpa and me. We met in a party. He was lonely and playing the piano in a room. I being a violinist joined in as well. And from then on our lives changed,"

"So does it mean it's a good omen?" I asked.

"I don't know. They say everything happens for a reason,"

"Whose they?" Christoff asked.

"The wise men and women,"

"Ah huh. I'm sure that includes you and Grandpa," he said.

Grandma gave a slight smile and said, "I know you two are young but believe me when I say, everything happens for a reason,"

"Nah," Christoff disapproved, "Life's random never pre-ordained,"

"And so should it be. One need not find reason in the chaos of life,"

"Grandma you don't mean that random things just fit in perfectly at the right time, do you?"

"I do. But only when you mould the shape of your life right, Christoff,"

"That's deep," I replied, "But the way you say it. It may be true,"

While we were talking, there was a knock at the door.

"I'll open it," I said.

"Lisa, what are you doing here?" said Trisha as she stood on the porch with August holding a gift.

"I'm here with Christoff," I replied, "Please come in,"

They both entered in and were greeted with delight by Grandma.

"O! My little boy has grown so much," said Mary cuddling him.

"Happy birthday," the child replied giving her the gift.

"Thank you," she said.

She then looked at Trisha before speaking, "You arrived just a bit late to hear the melody,"

Trisha was a bit surprised, "Who played it?"

"These two did," she said facing towards us.

"Really," she said looking at me.

"Yes, a bit," I replied.

Trisha then looked at Christoff and gave a smile.

"Can I have a word with you, Christoff?" she asked him.

"Sure," said he as they left us. Meanwhile Grandma had gone upstairs leaving August, Luce and I seated on the sofa, with the boy remaining silent.

I thought it to be the perfect opportunity to talk to him about Eve, but was held back by another knock.

"This place is certainly busy today," I said before walking towards the door.

On the porch stood a cold man staring fixatedly at a letter in his hand.

"Who are you looking for?" I said to him.

"Christoff Myers. Is he here?"

"Well he's upstairs. You can wait for him inside. I'll go and call him,"

The visitor clumsily seated himself beside August with his eyes still gazing on that letter.

"That's good news, Trish,"

"They say he is recovering very fast. Maybe a couple of months more and he'll be back,"

"….I'm sorry for all the trouble,"

"Don't be. It wasn't your fault,"

As I entered the room I saw Christoff's sad face for a moment before it turned calm once more.

"There's a visitor asking for you,"

"For me?"

"He's waiting downstairs. You might wanna check on him,"

"Sure,"

When Christoff greeted him, the young man gave a wry smile and said, "You don't remember me, do you?"

"No. But from the package that you carry, I assume you work at the Barrows,"

"You're right. I'm Jack Grenings, the lead technician at the firm,"

"What's in it?"

"It's a gift from Mr. Jeffrey,"

"Mr. Jeff. That's interesting. That lazy moron has now become the manager?"

"Yes. Now if you may accept this, I may be disposed of my duties,"

"Seeing how giddy you look. Any specific instructions for me,"

"4 days. That's what he said,"

"Fantastic. Give Jeff my greetings,"

"Sure will," he said before leaving.

Meanwhile Trisha and Mary were conversing at the dining table. August sat alone at the settee, before I joined him.

"You know August,…" I had just begun before Christoff barged in.

"Not here," he said signaling me towards Mary. I understood and changed the topic.

"So who was that guy?"

"My office associate,"

"He looked nervous,"

"It's expected when you're already running late for a train journey,"

A few minutes had just passed before Mary called out to Christoff.

"You know, Trisha and I were thinking if you could take Lisa here and show her Shaira today,"

"Today? I'll tour her tomorrow," he replied.

"Yes, its fine," I joined in as well.

"Nope. I won't hear no. You'll take her straight to Isen's place, hire a brougham, and show her this town,"

"But today's your....."

Trisha interrupted him and said, "Just do it Christoff. You know Mary doesn't take no for an answer,"

The look in both of their eyes were so stern on Christoff that he finally complied. And off we were to Isen's.

Falling in Love

While we were walking all alone through the snow, silence prevailed between us. But that silence was too loud for me because strange thoughts had started entering my mind.

"Why's he so silent? Is he thinking about what Mary said? No that's not possible. Or is it that he....has he begun to like me?"

My mind felt cramped and I shrieked, "Stop it,"

Those words took Christoff by surprise.

"Are you alright?" he asked.

"....Yes , yes everything's fine," I stumbled in my words as I looked at him.

"You are not thinking about what Grandma said. Are you?" he said stopping.

That took me by surprise, "No, no absolutely no. I'll never fall for you,"

"I thought so," he said and started walking again.

This quiet walk with snow falling from above, and the wind making us shiver made me feel warm and I won't deny it now," I was starting to fall for him,"

"We're here," said Christoff while we stood before a small inn.

He knocked on the door and out came a middle-aged man with a French beard. He had a ruddy coarse face that complemented his burly body and a heavy voice. His eyes were drooping and an alcoholic smell emanated from his mouth as he slouched against the wall.

"You looking for something eh," he said off-handedly.

"Isen....Mary sent me here," said Christoff.

The moment he had heard that name, his eyes popped open, and his sloppy gait went straight upright. He looked at him and then poked him on the shoulder.

"Oh, my goodness. It's really you," he said aloud.

"Yeah, yeah, wash your face first and come out,"

Within no time, Isen was standing outside with us completely neat and clean both from his appearance and smell.

"I need a brougham and you of course. We're gonna tour Shaira,"

"El Pasio?" Isen asked.

"Yes,"

"Wait a minute here,"

Isen then went round the corner of the street, leaving us alone.

"El Pasio, it is a horse I guess?" I asked curious.

"You'll see, and by the way don't stare in his eyes," he said earnestly.

"Why?"

"Cause if you do, that perverted animal is gonna stalk you the rest of his life, unless it finds something more attractive,"

"Perverted horse, that's the first time I've heard that," I said laughing.

However all my laughter and humour were left spell-bound when I saw that creature. I've seen horses before, but never like this. It was black as night, its eyes were pale white with brown pupils and above all its hoofs were large and I dare say if I have ever seen a bigger horse. It drew the carriage with grace and elegance of a king. Behind it, in the driver's seat, was seated a completely opposite figure and believe me when I say that one's beauty is enhanced by the lesser beautiful ones.

"Hop in," Isen said as he stopped the brougham.

We entered in and found ourselves seated in plush green cushion seats, with glass windows on both sides and the back as well.

"To Jericho Garden," said Christoff to Isen sliding the little wood outlet in front.

"A garden, in winter. I doubt it'd be worth our trip," said I.

"It's more than a garden," he said smilingly.

And off we rode.

It sounds strange in the 21st century to find a brougham and even stranger to find yourselves riding in one. But that is Shaira's beauty, it's a very rare place that you can find.

While we sat inside the carriage, streams of wooden house passed us, until the land became more steeper, and we found ourselves ascending a slope. We talked throughout the journey, but never once did he speak about himself. Some time passed before we arrived at this mystical place.

I alighted down and saw a large wooden house named Jericho Garden. Its outlook disappointed my good spirits and I said

"It's not a garden I see, but a large ordinary house,"

"You're impatient. Just walk inside," Christoff said, "And you , Isen park the brougham and join us as well,"

I trudged along the path that led to the house and opened its door. It was dark inside and one could hardly see anything.

I stood there before Christoff and Isen joined in.

"There's nothing here," I said.

"Okay, just wait. Isen, turn the mirror," he said.

Isen went into the left corner and disappeared completely.

"What's he doing?" I asked

"Directing the light,"

As soon as he had finished, a great dazzle of gleam illuminated the gigantic room. And there it stood. Numerous, varied coloured trees and plants. But they were not ordinary ones. Each one of them were crafted to reality with great care. That is to say they were made entirely of glass.

"Behold the Glass Garden of Jericho," Christoff said aloud.

Stunned I was and yet there it lay in front of me.

I walked on the path that lay covered in some stone that kept glowing as I moved past illuminating the path in front of me..

"What's this? Some sensor," I asked.

"No, every step you take turns a lever that brings a coloured glass slab beneath this transparent floor."

I cared little for the answer, because when I touched the dazzling brown bark of a tree, a squirrel moved past my hand..

"Ah...something moved," I exclaimed.

"Don't worry its also made of glass, and run by pulleys embedded inside that bark."

Everywhere I saw, I found shades of green, brown, red' and a hue of inexplicable colours.

Christoff then walked past me and plucked a glass flower that hung from a plant. He then walked towards me and said

"Hold it close to your heart,"

I did as he told me, and then all of a sudden the closed petals of the flower intricately opened into a red shining rose.

"How did that happened?" I asked.

"Jericho made this out of resonance. It receives your heartbeat, and then amplifies that sound to trigger the parts inside to bloom into a flower,"

"I'm really amazed. I'd never thought that this could exist,"

"But it does," he said and shouted aloud, "Isen, let it sparkle,"

All of a sudden, the ceiling made of wood disappeared and I could see the open sky. Birds were flying across and then suddenly at the end of the room, a lady appeared.

She was dressed like an angel. And her skin glowed like the sun. She spoke with love and beckoned towards me.

I moved curiously towards her and then it happened. Wings of glass appeared from her shoulders, and then the lights faded out. Only she sparkled in front, and she took off towards the sky and disappeared.

"How did you feel?" Christoff asked.

But I didn't answer.

"That's the Angel Of Shaira. It was made by Jericho for her wife. She's Shaira and this town is her legacy,"

"But how did that happen?" I asked dumb-founded.

"That I'm afraid I can't explain. Its something that no one ever can. Its an optical illusion some say, but no matter how many times I've seen it, I can't figure it out. Rather I'm made more certain it exists,"

"But the sky,"

"That. The wood ceiling is a fake. Its made of glass. When I told Isen. to let it sparkle, I meant to direct the lights towards that. From outside it looks like wood but its glass,"

"The birds. The Angel flew, I saw it myself,"

That's when Isen appeared from the darkness, and said, "Its hallucinogens. The Angel was initiated by this house, when the real ceiling appeared,"

"Well that's it," said Christoff "You can walk around and see other things, but the main show's just over,"

"Maybe it's over but I would have loved to take some pictures of these things," I sighed.

"You know,...Your mind is the greatest canvas that God gave, and every time you see something new, it get's painted mysteriously,"

This comment of his evoked a rare word from me.

"Wow,...." I replied but paused momentarily.

"Wow, what?" he asked curious.

"No," I smiled and said, "It's just that I never thought that such a...... farcical bungler like you could sound like a philosopher," I said teasing.

This should have piqued him a bit, I thought, but instead he jousted back.

"You know, what we call people who philosophize over farcical things like a bungler,"

"No..." I replied curious, awaiting an answer

Instead he simply opened the door and walked off. I followed him as well and what happened next is hilarious.

"What's the answer?" I called out to him.

"A reporter," he chuckled back and kept walking.

"You fool....." I replied tingling but he wasn't going to stop and I wasn't going to calm down.

"What can I do to make him stop?" I pondered for a while.

.....Just then a bulb lit in my head, and my eyes sparkled like a child.

And then, I called out to him, "Christoff...."

No sooner did he turn round towards me and said, "Now what.." than I threw a snowball straight at him

And, "Whack," it him in the face and he shivered in agony, while I laughed my heart out.

"Who's a bungler now?" I said teasing.

However in reply, he greeted me with my own device.

Gathering the snow around, he dashed towards me as he got his snowballs prepared for the attack.

I on the other hand was surprised at his quickness, and ran around seeking cover.

Turning around , I looked backwards and "Whew,". A snowball flew past over my head.

"Can't even hit a target," I shouted out to him still evading.

This mouse and cat chase continued for a while, until I was finally able to outrun him and conceal myself behind the brougham.

A few minutes later Christoff came running around the corner, but found nobody in the vicinity. He walked around surveying the area but ultimately gave up clueless, and walked towards El Pasio.

"She's lucky," he mumbled to the gullible horse, while I stood there at the back. He then turned away from my direction and started looking towards the house, trying to catch his breath.

That's when I found the opportunity, to sneak around the horse with my tippy-toe feet.

I was only a feet away from him, and was just about to smash the snowball on his head, when all of a sudden a warm breath whispered at the back of my ear and a gentle push nudged me at the back. I felt a creeping sensation on my neck and gave a sudden shout before I lost all balance.

Christoff turned round and in that split second I stumbled down onto him.

There I landed on top of him as my face collided against his. He gave a cry of pain as one should when someone elbows you onto your stomach. At that moment our gazes were interlocked and his heartbeat resonated with mine. My body felt nervous and as I pulled my face back, my tresses entangled his face. I tried to get up, but again was pushed forward. And so once more I fell down, but this time with my lips tightly clenched, I ended up....kissing him on the lips.

He must have cried in agony had he the chance. For his jaws must have really hurt just like mine did. But as it all happened, we both found ourselves lying on the snow, in that awkward situation which was only compounded by El Pasio, who stood above us caressing my hair with his muzzle.

As I lay on top of Christoff clueless about this fact, he pushed me sideways and I landed hard on my face.

"Oooh....so it's this cold," I remarked in icy pain.

Meanwhile Christoff slapped the peeking horse on the right saying, "You perverted horse...You can't even handle the scent of a lady,"

But just like a true pervert would the horse didn't give a response. Instead it turned all his attention towards me as it caressed me on the arms.

"Christoff..." I said meekishly.

"Told you not to give him an incentive. But no.... you girls never listen," he said getting up.

"Wait here, I'll go and get Isen," he said and started off.

"No...don't leave me like this...," I shouted back before the horse caressed me on the face.

"You're much safer with that perverted horse than with a blood hound," he replied before walking off.

A moment or two passed before Isen entered the scene and took the horse away.

Christoff extended his arm and I grabbed it as he pulled me up.

"He's really....a perverted animal," I said dumb-founded.

"Did he do anything?" He said teasing.

"Obviously not," I said haughtily.

"My goodness. He didn't do anything..." he said joking, "I thought that your Channel perfume would have proved irresistible to him.....Damn the horse is decent than any man I know,"

"Very funny," I said as I alighted up the brougham.

Martini Effect

"Where are we going now?" I asked Christoff as we left Jericho Garden behind.

"Aren't you feeling hungry?" he asked.

"Yes, I'm famished....So are we going somewhere to eat?"

"Yup. It's an Inn. Located just a bit far from here,"

"What's its name?" I asked curious.

"You'll find out when we reach there," he said with a mysterious smile.

Thus, our little adventure sprawled out into wider realms and as we talked, one thing always troubled me. It meandered at the back of my mind, until finally I said it out.

"Christoff,....." I spoke with hesitation.

"Yes..." he said turning towards me.

However I couldn't get those words out. Maybe I felt a bit embarrassed. But that's when he helped me out.

"If it's about that kiss, then forget about it. It was just an accident," he said casually.

His remark eased my nervousness a bit and I replied with confidence, "You're right....Besides I will never fall for you,"

"But.......you will fall on me," he said punning my sentence.

"Hey... that was an accident....I don't have any feelings for you," I retaliated.

"Neither do I. But one question. Did you put any lipstick today?" he asked.

"Yes I did, why?"

"Because my mouth tastes like strawberry right now," he said smiling.

This remark evoked a rare feeling in me. It was of temper. Yet it brought a strange happiness on my face.

"Smile all you can because it's never happening again," I told him and turned towards the window.

"I know," he replied, "Let's move on,"

We passed over a little over-bridge and had transcended the snow covered meadows, which were lined by yew tress, before coming to a halt.

Christoff alighted down and I followed him in his steps. As we stood there on that narrow road, a dense forest lay towards us on our left while a small meagre looking inn lay on the right.

"Is this the place?" I asked.

"Yup," he smiled.

As we approached forward, traversing the stone laid path, a signpost could be seen.

"The Rum Pot Inn," I read the letters aloud while Isen had already entered in.

"Yup this is where you'll find all the drunkards of Shaira," said Christoff.

"Wait," I said coming to a halt, "I am not going in,"

"Why?"

"Why you ask. Why would I walk to a place where men swoon their lives in alcoholic smell,"

"Fine then, stay here..." he said walking off.

"Yes I will," I replied adamant.

"...And.....wait for the hungry wolves that come here looking for food. I bet they can't resist strawberry," he said in a scaring tone.

Before I could reply, a howling cry resounded the surrounding and filled the air with morose sorrow.

The moment I heard it I rushed forward towards Christoff's side.

"On second thought, drunkards ain't that bad people," I replied.

"Liar," he told me.

We stood on the wooden porch, and peered into the open door as a spectacle unfolded in front of us.

Two men were involved in a brawl, and were fighting it out. Bets were being placed at the counter, and beer jugs were flying high.

"She belongs to me," said the ruffian.

"No...she's mine," the other replied.

And bang they shook hands in a very civil manner, and knocked each other. The mob cheered them on, and as we were about to enter in, they all went silent, everyone staring at us.

The ruffians halted midway holding there untidy collars, while people had paused halfway while drinking.

"What's going on? Why are they staring at us?" I whispered in Christoff's ear.

"They aren't staring at us. But at you," he replied.

"Me?" I exclaimed.

"Yes, you're the second lady that these rum-pots have seen in their lives,"

"Second? I wonder who the firs...," I chuckled but stopped midway.

A strikingly pretty woman walked towards us dressed in red. She was fair to say the least, and her tresses adorned her beautiful face in shimmering cascading curls. She wore a frock, and I daresay I have ever seen anyone more lascivious yet elegant in my entire life.

"Boys call off the fight," she said in a commanding voice and everyone obeyed.

Then she stood in front of us and faced Christoff looking at her with those killer green eyes, "Whose she?" she said in her charming voice.

"She's a friend,"

"Friend..." she said with a gleam in her eyes, "And may I know what brings you here?"

"I heard today you were serving free drinks," he said confidently.

"Free? When did you become a drunkard?"

"Just today.... Now Isabell, let's finish the nuptial talks," he said affably and smiling.

The lady's expression suddenly changed friendly and she took us both by the arms and led us in.

"Free drinks to all," she shouted aloud, and a roar exploded in the house.

As I entered in, I realized that the Inn was much bigger than I had expected it to be. Both in name and size. It sprawled around on the linoleum, and wooden stairs leading to the first floor were lined by teak-wood bannisters. The walls were plastered red, and a dimly lit light added to Inn's charm, which was only enhanced by the lovely slow-moving music, that serenaded into your ears and tranquiled the vicinity.

People, both men and women, were having a wonderful time at their tables, as they talked about and laughed or rather smiled. They weren't drinking. Instead eating well-cooked food, and listening to good music.

"I thought you said that this was a place for drunkards," I told Christoff as the lady led us upstairs.

"Well it is, but not all of it. Only a part of the ground floor meets the criteria....Do you know the meaning of Rum-Pot?" he said.

"Literally it means alcohol, but figuratively I think it means friends... Good friends," I said after pondering for a while.

"Yup. This Inn is owned by Isabell Foster, the lady you see, walking ahead of us,"

"Is she a friend of yours?" I said as we walked along a large corridor before entering an alleyway.

"Keep following me," the lady said turning towards us.

"....Yes she is. And she's the one who keeps order in this inn," Christoff whispered in a low voice.

" Wow, a pretty lady like her can handle such ruffians. But how?" I asked curious.

"Don't go on her looks. I know she's hot. But not in that sense. Back when we were kids, she used to beat the persons up, who used to bully us, with a...."

But before he could speak further, a door opened in, and we found ourselves in a gigantic hall.

In front of us, there stood, a podium, right at the extreme back, where a band was playing a romantic upbeat tune. Just a bit ahead of the stage, there was a big platform, where you could see people waltzing in rhythm. The ceiling was decorated by myriad dim-lights that criss-crossed each other forming a darting pattern. As we looked towards our side, we noticed people sitting at the white gowned roundtables, and enjoying a happy meal.

"Welcome to the Boulevard," said Isabell.

"It's......" I gaped for a while in amazement and spoke, "Beautiful,"

She then led us to our seats, and disappeared into a side door leaving us two behind.

"Well...I never thought from its outlook, that this Inn was so enchanting," I told Christoff.

"Well...that was our plan when we first laid its foundation,"

"Wait...you built this place," I asked surprised.

"Yup, Isen, Isabell, and I. The three of us. We are childhood friends... When we first came here, Shaira lacked a proper dining place, and a drinking one as well. So that's when we decided to build this place.... The name Kum-Pot Inn as you see, is named after we three friends,"

"But why the simple exterior?"

"To keep away unnecessary attention. If you live in the city, then you should know this. A place is as beautiful as long as it isn't commercialized,"

"...It's true," I replied.

A few minutes later, Isabell entered into the scene and joined us as well. The food was served in, and it's aura seemed delicious and mouth-watering.

"You know, I'm wondering where Isen is seated. He entered in first, didn't he?" I asked.

"He's a sober fellow. The rum is his dearest buddy. He won't leave downstairs and come up here," Isabell told smiling.

"Yup," Christoff nodded his head in agreement.

"So Lisa.....you're a reporter?" Isabell asked.

"Yes...'

"Were you able to film those birds?"

"Nope... But Christoff said he would help me see them,"

"Help, and he. Really Christopher," she said looking at him with peering eyes.

He on the other hand was engrossed in his food. And when he looked up, those cooked spaghetti noodles were hanging from his mouth.

We both laughed at this, before he swooped the remaining in and asked innocently, "What happened?"

"Nothing....But how's everything going?" said Isabel.

"Fine...Like always...." he replied.

"Fine. 4 years Christoff, and it's fine..." she asked solemnly.

That comment of hers got me curious and I listened intently to their conversation.

"Don't start it now, Isabell," he said still eating.

"You can't go on like that..."

"I can...Besides" he said changing the topic, "Did you cook the food?"

At this Isabell gave a sad sigh and replied, "Yes....Isn't it good?"

"No....I thought after so many years, you would have really improved. But it's still..." he paused deliberately.

"Still what?" she asked haughtily.

"Still good.... And I'm glad that you haven't changed," he said looking at her.

"Neither have you," she said smiling.

The moment those two looked at each other, I noticed a chemistry between them. However it was one-sided.

Christoff thereafter left us for the washroom while we continued our conversation.

"You like him," I asked Isabell

"Yes....but only as a dear friend,"

"So what was it that you were talking about earlier?"

"Nothing...It's just the past," she tried to avoid the topic and I realized as well.

A minute later the music stopped and the lights went off. Then suddenly the limelight fell onto the podium and a couple made their way onto the stage.

"Ladies, and gentleman," they said in unison, "We request you all to stand up and make your way into the doors that our assistant show you to. There you will be given a dress each, and please wear that. It's for an event that we are organizing. And its gonna start shortly,"

Everyone who heard this were a bit confused. But that's when Isabell, got up from her seat and taking a mic announced, "Everyone, please enter your doors,"

The next moment, I found the people leaving the hall and as they did the tables were being cleared out of the room.

"What's all this for?" I asked her.

"Today's a special day," she smiled at me and taking me by the arm, led me through a door into a small room.

"Wait," I said coming to a halt, "What's all this commotion for?"

But she didn't answer. Instead, she handed me a bag.

"What's in this?" I asked.

"Open that and wear it," she said in a sprightly voice.

As I opened it, I gave a cry of amazement.

In front of my eyes stood a beautiful white gown. It was full sleeved and had a silken body. Light, and coloured like the dove, it drooped down in a cascade pattern, having a high back. To sum it all up, it was exquisite.

"Wear it," said Isabell again.

I did as she asked and within five minutes, I was standing in front of a mirror with Isabell arranging my hair into braids and curls.

"How do I look?" I asked her.

"Beautiful," she said smiling, "But wait something's missing. Ah here it is,"

She gave me a matching pair of stunning sandals and said, "Perfect. Let's roll out,"

As I opened the door, and stepped out, a lucid darkness greeted me. I walked forward a bit, but that's when it all happened.

Suddenly a light fell on my face, and as I looked towards its direction, a voice mellowed out into the hall saying this aloud,

"Ladies and gentleman, please welcome.... Miss Lisanna Sparks,"

That's when all the lights turned on, blinding me and I saw the outline of people looking at me as they said in unison,".....Happy Birthday, Lisanna,"

That's when my gaze fell onto the stage and I saw Christoff, still dressed in his usual clothes, smiling at me.

Isabell walked out from the back and holding my arm, she took me towards the podium.

"Come with me," she spoke in a whisper.

As I made my way towards the stage, a red carpet had been laid, while a welcoming music was being played. Finally when I ascended those steps and stood before the mic, I took a deep breath and said,

"Thank you. Thank you everybody,"

Christoff then walked towards my side and holding the mic announced," Okay guys,.. let the party begin,"

No sooner this announcement was made than a rocking, and grooving music erupted the roof of the hall. All the lights went back dim, and the people around started dancing.

"How did you find out?" I asked in a soft voice.

"Your mother had called this morning while you were sleeping. And as you have the habit of recording incoming calls with your cell phone, I just happened to hear one of it," said Christoff.

"And just to let you know, it was Grandma who planned all this out. Not me,"

"...Still then, thank you," I told Christoff.

While we were talking, Isabell made her way up the stage and said, "Why are you two talking? Go down there and dance,"

"Well, I don't think, I can in this gown," I replied.

At this, she made a knowing glance at Christoff and he replied, "Come on....don't look at me. You do this,"

"Nope....If you don't, I'll call Mary....." she said in a grave voice.

"Fine....No need to use her every time...." he said with a sigh.

After that Isabel took a few steps away from me and I asked her puzzled, "What happened?"

But that's when Christoff lit a cigarette lighter and showed the flame towards the white gown that was drooping onto the floor.

I gave a cry of surprise as my dress caught fire. This in turn caught the crowd's attention and they looked at me, baffled.

No,..... I was not burning. Instead, just like you light a paper at its one corner, and it withers away slowly in the flame, my white gown got burnt away as the flame slowly inched towards my toe. The drapes that were once on the floor no longer remained.

While the flame traversed over my legs, my white dress began to turn red and continued to burn away but this time in a pattern. Starting from a feet above my left toe, the flame whirled in direction and continued obliquely round in a spiral helix till it reached some inches above my right knee. Thereafter, it curled backwards, slithering up my back shoulder, and flaming away the high back end, revealing my shoulder blade. It then arched towards my neck, and descended down my hands, burning away all the sleeves. Finally as my gown was turning red from below, the smouldering flame arched over my chest, all the while turning my dress into a stunning red oblique skirt, till it finally extinguished at the helm of my neck, where my locket was hanging.

"Voila....It's done," said Christoff as everybody clapped their hands in applause.

My white gown, in that spurt of a moment, had transformed into a vivacious red oblique skirt, both sleeveless and with a low back end. With its spiral helix at the knee, my legs were exposed to public scrutiny, while I stood there clueless.

Isabell walked over to me and whispered into my ear, "Feeling nervous?"

"Yes....How do I look?" I asked her.

"Smoking hot and ready to kill," she said with a smile.

Christoff then took the mic and said to musicians to play the upbeat and grooving Venetian tune.

He then walked over to me and offered his hand asking, "Wanna dance, Miss Sparks?"

"...Yes...." I said in hushed tone, accepting his hand.

There we descended down the stairs, and made our way to the dance floor while everyone kept staring at us.

"I don't like this. They are staring at us," I told Christoff as he held me by the waist and we mooned along in fast steps.

"Not us. But you," he said before whirling me away from him and pulling me back.

I came back towards his arms clueless as to what he meant. Then clasping his left hand with mine and holding me by the waist on the right, he turned around me and exchanged a quick word," You look beautiful,"

"Do I?" I asked doubtful. But instead of replying he bended me towards the floor, till my right leg stood pointing in mid-air. Then he leaned forward towards me till inches remained between us, and stood there staring into my eyes.

As he held me in that tranceless swoon, everyone had started eyeing us. However he didn't care. He simply kept looking at me.

"Christoff....pull me back...." I whispered hurriedly. He didn't answer.

"Christoff, do you hear m..." But before I could complete my sentence he suddenly pulled me back. Then holding me by the waist, he tossed me up in the air.

I gave a slight cry as I was in mid air. Then as I descended down, I closed my eyes and the music stopped all at once.

A second later when I opened them, I saw red and white balloons flying everywhere in the hall. Then I turned my gaze towards the front and noticed Christoff holding me in his grip, with his arms nestled around my waist.

"Time, to cut the cake," he said and lowered me down.

"Thank you," I replied with my cheeks turning pink.

"You're welcome," he said and left me among the encircling crowd with the cake in the centre.

"That's the first time since Yew that I have seen a true smile on your face," said Isabell as we stood round a corner.

"Yes, she's right, Christoff," said Isen who had just joined in.

"Maybe you're right....But still, that changes nothing," I told them.

"Nothing huh. That word speaks everything," she replied.

The cake was cut and the songs recited. Fervour and enthusiasm gripped the Boulevard and when finally it all ended, it was time for us to leave Rum-Pot Inn.

"Thank you for the hospitality," I said to Isabell.

"You're always welcomed, Lisa" she replied.

"As are we right?" said Christoff joking.

"Yup but it applies only to Isen..... And as for you, don't show me your face until you find yourself a soulmate...." she said with a really scary voice.

"If I do, then..." he said teasing.

" Then ....I'll smash that smile off your handsome face with my hockey stick,"

"....Wow that's deeply consoling," Christoff replied before saying goodbye.

Frozen Falls

As we rode in our carriage, a few minutes passed before I plundered Christoff with all my curious questions and he answered them with patience.

"So how is it, that the red dress I'm wearing now, got created out of the flame you lit?"

"It's called Martini Effect....That white gown that Isabell gave you was made up of 2 layers. The inner one was the red oblique skirt, that you are wearing , while the outer one was made up of flash paper. Not ordinary ones but made of silken paper....Back then, when I lit the flame, I showed it only to exterior layer. Its ignition point was reached and it disappeared into thin air revealing the actual dress,"

"Wow, that's ingenious. But what would have happened if you had shown the flame to the inner layer?" I asked.

"....I don't know.....But the effect would have been the same.... I mean if anything went wrong then you would have still lit the stage on fire....although literally,"

"What? I could have been burnt..." I asked surprise.

"No.....I had taken precautions," he said assuredly.

"Precautions?"

"Yes, I had a fire extinguisher, ready by the stage," he said joking.

".....Very funny...You're lucky it all went well," I replied with sternness.

"Yup lucky indeed,..."

"...So are we returning to Mary's home now?" I said changing the topic.

"Nope. There's still this one thing that you must see" said Christoff excited.

"What's that?" I asked.

"The Frozen Falls," he said.

It was late in the evening, almost night, when our journey reached its concluding stage. Isen had driven us through the Alpine rocks, that had some mysterious carvings on them, and then rode us across the Shaira Lake, for quite a fair distance before coming to a halt.

When we alighted down, I was so captivated by the Falls, that I forgot my jacket in the brougham, and hurriedly made my way out, in that flimsical red dress, that too in cold weather.

I feel it won't be exaggerating when I say that the Falls is the most outstanding place on Earth. It rises very high easily exceeding the world's highest towers. When you look at it, you see trickles of water frozen and forming pointed spikes. But it's grandeur lie in the Auroras that dance above it. Their reflections fall onto this Fall and it glimmers in a hue of rainbow.

"It's magnificent," I said.

"Well go ahead and touch the frozen waterfall," said Christoff.

As soon as I did, I realized something strange.

"It's warm," I said, "And wait I see shells inside it,"

"Those are the Juancos that failed to hatch. You see nature has strange ways to work. These shells they aren't wasted. Rather they solidify like magma does, and form gemstones. These in turn regulate the temperature of the Frozen Falls and Shaira lake helping the others to hatch."

I stood there on the frozen river for sometime, while Christoff and Isen stood there talking near the brougham. Half an hour or so passed like this, with me admiring the work of nature. However it was getting late and reluctantly I began to leave.

But that's when the ground shook and the ice cracked. I heard the horse's scream, and found the pointed spikes falling down. I ran immediately but it proved fatal. My leg slipped and I came crashing down onto the ice. It broke and the now active water fall sent me moving downstream.

I gave a scream as the ice on which I stood broke and I fell into the freezing water. I was being washed downhill with a great current and was headed towards a cliff. My head crashed against an ice mass and I lost all my senses.

The Rider

"hat was that?" asked Isen.

"Earthquake," I exclaimed in horror.

"O no!" he said turning. But there was no time to be lost.

I unbridled the horse from the brougham and took off.

"Isen, follow me if you can," I shouted.

"Yes, you go ahead," he said gravely.

The bank was not idle for running a horse because of ice. But El Pasio did good.

Beside me the river was gushing forward with tremendous velocity and Lisa's scream had inundated my ears.

But what frightened me was the silence that followed.

"Come on boy, faster," I commanded.

I could not see her for quite some distance but then I caught glimpse of her. She was senseless and was flowing straight towards the cliff.

I didn't have any rope to support me, so there was only one option. The bank was very wide, but Lisa was nearer to my end. I had to jump to get to her.

While the horse ran as fast as he could, I stood up on it, with my left leg slightly crouched at my heels and my right knee touching my chest. Then I waited to time the jump.

"Now," I told myself and up I sprang straight down into the swirling water and the seething foam.

"Lisa......Lisa," I said grasping her by the arm and pulling her towards me. But there was no answer.

Now only one little trouble remained. "Now what? There's the cliff."

The river kept pushing us forward, and damn it was cold. I tried to swim across but to no avail.

All hopes seemed to fade. We kept drifting, and were now only a minute from the cliff.

But I saw a stone rock jutting just before the edge. I swam across along with the current and grasped the rock in my elbow with all my might. I guess we stood there against the pounding water for five minutes or so. But I was running out of strength. My fingers were losing grip, and so was my elbow.

Out of the deadly hissing of the river came a familiar voice, "Here grab this," Isen shouted throwing a rope towards me. Damn if anybody on earth is more unlucky, just ask him if he ever experienced this. The rope fell inches away from my reach.

I let go of the rock and plunged forward, but my wet hands slipped and Lisa was about to fall.

"No,...." I exclaimed and with my left hand holding the rope, I grappled for hold of her.

I caught her by her fingers, interlocked hers with mine, and embraced her against me as Isen tried to pull.

One thing good about Isen, is this, "He's stupid. And know what, all stupid persons are headstrong in what they do,"

He pulled us like the Hulk and out of the river into the safety of the bank. We were now out of the river but an immediate danger lay against us now. Lisa's head was injured, she was bleeding and to compound to that hypothermia was evident. The only good thing was that she hadn't drowned.

My own body was giving in to the cold, and I could barely walk.

"Isen," I spoke in a whispering tone, "take the horse and ride her through the woods and straight to Grandma's home. Trisha's there, she'll help out,"

"But what about you?" he asked.

"Don't you see Isen the brougham can't drive through the woods," I said in a raised voice, "Time is of essence my friend. Go now. I'll be fine."

My voice was never more loud and clear. Isen alighted the horse, and rode off with Lisa hurriedly.

Meanwhile I attempted to walk towards the brougham. But it didn't work. I just tripped, and fell down.

Lying on my face, with snow falling over, my life force was draining. I thought it was a far, far better rest I was going to than I could have ever imagined. With this, I closed my eyes finally.

Two Lives

"Come on, Pasio. Run, faster" I commanded.

We crossed the woods, and were now on the main road. Adrenaline was running high. Who would have thought that such a beautiful day would turn into a nightmare?

Two lives were at stake. One of Miss Lisa and the other of Christoff's. And I could only save one. My job was to get her to safety, but leaving a friend behind never hurt more. I just hope he will hold on until I return. But with each passing second, my hopes were waning.

We crossed the by-lanes, the alleyways, the frosted fields and kept riding till I saw a glimpse of Mary's home. We arrived at her door in blistering speed. The horse took some stopping, but it did fine. Getting Miss Lisa off, I knocked at the door hurriedly.

"Isen...., Lisa.." said Mary in terror as she looked at the blood flowing from her head.

I got her inside the house and met Trisha who immediately attended to her.

"Where's Christopher?" asked Mary worriedly.

"He's out on the Frozen Falls. He jumped into the river to save her...I'll explain later but I must go..." and I left recklessly on my horse.

"Hold out buddy," I prayed, and rode to the Falls.

"Is she going to be alright?" Mary asked pensively.

"Yeah, I have cleaned and wrapped her wound. She needs warmth, otherwise hypothermia is evident, and Grandma..." said Trisha.

"Yes..."

"Boil some water. I'll pour that into a pouch and place it over her quilt. That should do for now,"

She did as Trisha told, and Lisa was now laying on the couch unconscious.

"I'm more worried about Christoff, Grandma," said Trisha, "He jumped into the icy waters, and is now lying somewhere near the Falls. And the time that it took Isen to come here, it could prove fatal,"

"I value your advice as a doctor. But don't worry about him, he'll return save, I believe," Mary said in a comforting manner, but even she knew the risk Christoff was in.

Pandemonium

"Giving up already!" a voice whispered to me.

"Hosse, "

"Yes, Christoff. Get up,"

"I can't,"

"Why?"

"I don't know,"

"I know. It's because of guilt, isn't it?"

"....Yes,"

"Well a person who would die saving a loved one isn't guilty,"

"No, it happened because of me,"

"Stop it here. You love them. Don't you?"

"Yes,"

"Then live for them...Never give up," The voice said and faded.

I slowly opened my eyes. I was cold, and weak. I tried getting up, but my body wouldn't comply. However that voice made me realise, that I had a responsibility. I couldn't die, not yet.

I thus pushed my hands against the snow. But I fell down on my face.

"Try again," I urged myself.

Slowly, I got up, but my numb feet tumbled me down.

"Try, try again," I shouted in agony as I forced myself up.

I moved forward a bit, and fell down hard. This struggle didn't get easy. I tried and failed. Again I tried, and failed. But I didn't give up. Finally after a long fight against my body I got up and walked towards the place where the brougham was parked.

There I sat down on the brougham's footsteps, and breathed heavily. The cold glass window condensed. I wiped the drops off, and caught a glimpse of a jacket.

"It's Lisa's," I told myself, and searched her pockets for anything that could help me.

It was then I caught hold of a peculiar looking needle.

It had an insulated wooden base with a push button. Its ends were pointed and on the wooden cover were written in minute letters, "Do not stab,"

My vision was starting to get blurry again. I had to make a choice. I could wait for Isen to return before which in all probability I'd be dead, or I could use this thing.

It took some pondering, but then I made up mind. I pressed the push button and holding it down, I stabbed myself in the chest. Suddenly a wringing sound whispered into my ear, and my body felt a tingling sensation. The pain never eased, but before I realized, I fell asleep.

Awakening

My mind felt heavy, and I could barely see. However I remembered falling into the river. I tried to move my hand, but only my fingers responded with a wiggle.

"You're awake," said a familiar voice, "Don't talk now. Take rest,"

Those words gave me comfort and I opened my eyes completely to see Trisha by my bedside.

"Trisha, how am I here?" I asked in whispering tone.

"Christoff saved you," she said.

"He did. Where's he?" I asked curious.

"He's asleep,"

"O...How long have I been like this?"

"A day and a half," she said

"That's bad, my time here will come to an end tomorrow,"

"You got to leave?"

"Yes,"

"I just hoped to see the Juancos, but that seems a dream now,"

"Don't worry, when Christoff's awake I'll tell him,"

"Thank you,"

She left me in the room where I laid in the bed for another day. The next morning when I had regained some strength, I got up wearily and walked to the hallway.

I stood there for some time but found nobody. There I saw a light falling on the floor from a half closed room. I walked towards it, and when I entered the room, I found Trisha injecting Christoff with some serum as he lay asleep. Grandma sat in a chair by his bedside, and Isen stood in a corner.

My expression was one of guilt and sadness. Christoff was in such a pitiable condition that I could barely describe him.

"It happened because of me," I said with my voice cracking.

Tears had started rolling down my eyes, and I couldn't wrestle myself against them.

"If he hadn't,.. then he would have been alright,"

"Don't say that, and don't you cry," said Grandma as she hugged and consoled me.

"It wasn't your fault. He's like that. He'd do anything for a loved one," she told me.

"Yes. Christoff's like that. If you blame yourself, you're demeaning the efforts he took to save you," said Trisha.

All the while Isen stood in that corner and never uttered a word.

I walked towards him and I could see the worry in his eyes.

"I'm sorry Isen...." I said to him.

"Don't be. If it wasn't for you he wouldn't be alive,"

"...For me,"

"Yes. I found this thing in his chest and your jacket near him. He stabbed himself with this,"

He handed me my pocket stun gun and said, "The electric shock kept his heart beating,"

I didn't answer but sat by the bedside and looked at him.

"If you look after him, we'll go and prepare some food," said Trisha.

"Yes," I told her.

"Isen you too come," said Grandma.

And they left closing the door behind.

He lay asleep but his face was never more expressive. An innocence showed in him and his brevity, no that's not apt, his recklessness to save me, was evident from his wounds.

I put my palm on his face, and caressed him.

"He's saved me twice," I pondered, "And he did it without a reason,"

"Who am I to him? I'm a complete stranger, yet he put his life in jeopardy for me,"

"I on the other hand, had been entangled by his innocence and his care for his loved ones. Grandma did try to tell me about his past, but I didn't care about it now. To me his present was what I was interested in,"

Emotions took the better of me, I couldn't help but lean towards his face and kiss him. The moments our lips were locked, I closed my eyes and a tear drop fell over his face that lay encircled by my hair. I wished for the time to stop, for this feeling of warmth and comfort to never end, but that was not to be.

While we kissed his eyes gradually opened and saw my face. I pulled back and heard him say, "Lisa....you're safe."

On one hand I had to let go of that feeling but on the other I was never more happy in my entire life.

I didn't care to wipe my tears away. I simply smiled and said, "Yes, we are awake,"

"How's...."

I put my finger on his lips and said, "Don't talk now, rest. I'll come back in a minute,"

I left the room ecstatic and went downstairs into the kitchen, "He's awake," I said merrily.

Those words lit up their worried faces, and we rushed upstairs to see him.

They all greeted him in delight and he talked, as if nothing had happened. Afterwards he whispered something in Isen's ear. It brought a smile on their faces. His chest hurt a bit as he laughed but he didn't stop.

"Let's go to the dining table and eat," Christoff said to everybody.

"No... you stay here," we all said in unison.

"Nope. I won't. Today's Lisa last day here. Let's not spend it idly. Isen get me up."

Our insistence was futile, and Isen and I supported him as we went downstairs.

Luce who was lying by the fire saw Christoff and rushed towards him.

He told us to leg go of him as he squatted down and patted her.

August was sitting by the dining table, and he too hugged Christoff, "Thank you. It worked,"

Christoff gave a smile and said, "You're welcome kiddo,"

It was simple food but I can shout it out to the entire world that this is the best food one can ever have.

"Family, that's what this is huh," I pondered.

We talked about the triflest of things and laughed at our own mistakes. Everyone shared something from their past, but not Christoff. He stayed aloof on that matter, and would occasionally smile.

After the lunch, Isen started to leave and I escorted him outside the door.

"Thank you," he said.

"You're welcome..." I replied cheerily.

He turned and walked some steps before I called him out, "Isen, can you tell me something?"

"Yes, ask what you may," he said.

"What did Christoff tell you about back in that room?"

His face lit up and he laughed before saying, "Oh that. He told me that he found a childhood picture of yours in the jacket,"

"That's the reason for your laugh,"

"No, no he said that you looked like a squirrel with a broken front teeth,"

"He told you that!" I exclaimed, "I'm going to get that smart alec,"

"Be easy on him," said Isen and I bid him goodbye.

Farewell

I entered in and sat next to Christoff by the fire. Grandma and Trisha were talking at the table and August was upstairs playing with Luce.

"I look like a squirrel," I told him a bit ticked off.

"O no. Not at all," he replied in surprise.

"With a broken front tooth," I continued.

"No, it looked good on you,"

"Good. That's the reason why you laughe..."

Before I could finish Christoff had started running upstairs.

"Wait you fool," I said running after him.

"Oh you were right they quarrel just like kids," I heard Trisha telling Grandma.

Nevertheless, I continued and we entered the room running.

Christoff went round the bed to the other side, and stopped there.

"Listen, I didn't mean to...." he said as I picked up a pillow.

I ran round the corner but he hurried across trampling the bed," Lisa, calm down...."

However that was not going to happen. I too jumped onto the bed and ran across it. But my feet slipped and I came crashing down on to Christoff. The pillow flew off my hands and came tumbling down on to us. We both ended up onto the carpet that lay across the floor.

For the second time I lay on top of him with our face against each other. I could feel his heartbeat as he did mine. We stared and stared before Christoff caressed my drooping hair, against the back of my ear. There was that unusual silence that is always there, when you can't make up your own mind.

Then we both leaned against each other but before we could kiss I saw August standing at the door with Luce beside him.

I stood up in an instant, trampling down Christoff's knee and exclaimed, "August!"

The child was innocent but smart, "You two, please keep the doors closed," He told us before closing the door.

Christoff meanwhile had gotten up the bed and was nursing his knee.

"I'm sorry," I said to him.

"It's okay," He replied.

"Let us go downstairs," I said hurriedly.

"Yes,"

Without further ado, we both were now sitting by the fireside.

"I heard a loud noise upstairs," Grandma said ,"Is everything okay?"

"Yes," we said in unison and she smiled.

We sat silent for a while before Christoff spoke, "Okay now. Since today's your last day here, let's go to Shaira Lake,"

"You haven't fully recovered," I said.

"Says who. The one who was about to hit me with a pillow,"

"Yeah yeah, but I don't look like a squirrel,"

"No you don't. You look pretty, slim, fair and all the other adjectives. But I called you a squirrel because you are the most interesting, inquisitive person I have ever met in my life,"

"You mean like a squirrel,"

"Exactly,"

"Well then. I'm sorry,"

"Okay let's finish this nuptial talks. We are going out. Its 7 already. We should reach there by nine,"

As we told Mary and Trisha about our little journey, they both strangely agreed without complaining. The reason however I got to know as I was closing the door behind.

"As long as those two have each other, we've got nothing to worry," Mary told Trisha and I overheard.

While we were some distance off home, a voice called us from the back.

On turning we found August running towards us. He stopped and I noticed he was carrying a paper in his hand.

"Can you give this to her?" he said turning towards Christoff.

"Sure, now quickly go back, okay," he replied.

And off he returned.

Treading along we chatted about many things, one of which holds significance to this story.

"So her name is Eve," I said.

"Yeah, Evelyn," Christoff said smilingly.

"So what did you do?"

"Nothing. I just told him the words,"

"What words?"

"I'm August, can I be your friend?"

"That's all,"

"Nope. He was very nervous to speak those words, so he wrote it down, and gave it to her,"

"What did she say?"

"Yes. I'd like to be your friend. My name's Evelyn,"

"I can't believe it worked,"

"Yup it worked and they are friends,"

"And this letter he gave now,"

"Well let's read then,"

Only three kind words were written

"Happy Birthday Eve,"

"That's sweet," I said

"Yeah. Let's cut this topic, we'll give this to her when we arrive there."

It was 9 when we arrived at Shaira Lake that lay covered in mist. It had an eerie silence, but we both knew that the melody would soon spring this place to life.

"Here, hold my hand," said Christoff.

I did as he told me, and we advanced closer to the lake. Christoff meanwhile, took out a feather from his pocket and held it in his hand. We stood there waiting as time passed and I got impatient.

"Looks like they've left the place," I said.

"Patience. You really lack it," Christoff said.

Before I could reply a melody filled the vicinity, and our own body started glowing.

"It works," Christoff said.

"But this time there's no thunder," I asked.

"Nope. This is the festive of Shaira. The jubilant dance of the newborns."

All of a sudden glowing figures started darting out from the dark trees, and then up they flew, twinkling like the stars. Two birds from opposite directions winged past each other, and third one flew out of their intersection. There was a pattern to this, and in no time there stood the Angel, sparkling against the dark sky, that I saw at the Jericho Garden.

"It's Shaira," I exclaimed bedazzled.

"Yes. Jericho saw this and built that after his wife,"

The birds stood there for a minute or so before flying off in different directions. But two birds flew straight towards us. One was very small, and the other medium sized.

Christoff opened his right palm and the big one sat straight onto it. The small one however sat straight on my nose.

"Christoff...." I said in a hushed tone, a bit scared.

"Don't worry. They're remembering you,"

"Me?"

"Yup, these birds can remember faces. This big one here was small when it first stood right here in my palm some two years ago,"

"You can recognize it,"

"Yes, I put a small red string on its toe,"

These two birds then flew around us in a helix, and stopped in front of us.

"You can go now," Christoff said in a low voice and off they went.

Our body stopped glowing, and the mist cleared up gradually, and then we returned to Mary's home.

This spectacle had enraptured me, and I wished to stay forever in Shaira. But I couldn't, I had to leave. The next morning a sumptuous breakfast was prepared by Grandma to felicitate my departure. It was lovely and after that I began to take leave.

"If you're ever back in Shaira, do come and see us," said Trisha.

"Yes, and a very happy life to you," said Grandma merrily.

"Goodbye," said August.

"Where's Christoff?" I asked since I hadn't seen him since breakfast.

A brougham stood in front of Mary's home, and from it Christoff alighted down.

"Where have you been?" I said standing at the doorway.

"To my house. Your travel bag and other belongings were there. I thought it was better to bring them here,"

"Thank you," I replied.

I bade them goodbye and entered Isen's brougham. Christoff accompanied me and then we rode uphill to the lodgings where my assistant and car was.

Throughout the journey, no words were spoken. It seemed apt because we both didn't know then that what existed between us was love or friendship.

When the brougham pulled out, we alighted down and I thanked Isen for his help. And now came the most difficult part. Saying goodbye to the person for whom my feelings were justified but not certain.

We stood in front of each other completely silent. My eyes evidently showed my indecision but his were fathomless.

"Thank you for everything," I said at last.

"Anytime you come here, you're always welcomed," he said affably.

"I know,"

"So this is it,"

"Yes,"

"Then goodbye, Lisa."

I turned to leave but my mind didn't settle down. I had walked a few steps when I turned to see his back as he walked slowly towards the brougham.

"Christoff," I called out.

He turned immediately and said, "Anything wrong,"

"Yes, something big,"

"What's that?" he asked concerned.

"You,"

"Me?" he said confused.

"Yes,"

"What's wrong with me?" he said with a puzzled face.

"The roses. There in your frock coat. Is it for someone else?" I asked in an innocent voice.

He gave a smile and said, "O that. I forgot,"

He took it out and gave it to me.

"I brought this as a parting gift,"

"The Humming Roses," I said, "it symbolizes love you know, doesn't it?"

"No. Not exactly. It symbolizes reason. It reasons your actions. Depends on how you think...."

His expression was very much familiar to me. He didn't have an answer, so I helped him out.

"You don't have to answer now," I said interrupting him, "Until I return here again, let it be like that,"

"You sure,"

"Never more," I said embracing him

A cold wind had started flowing, and the clouds were getting darker. I kissed him on his cheek and said

"Goodbye, Christopher,"

"Goodbye Lisanna,"

That was our last conversation. It was full of awkwardness and a bit emotional. But thinking now, I wished to have said those three words. However, destiny had planned otherwise.

I thus left in my car with my assistant driving. Rain had started falling and I didn't look back, 'cause that would change my mind. And at last I bid adieu to Shaira.

Nostalgia

I flipped the cover and there in bold letters were printed, "Don't forget March 29,"

I turned the page around and found a letter inside it, "This I give to you. I can't write anymore. My conscience won't let me. P.S Yours Christopher," it said.

From page 1, it was clear it was his memoir. I started reading it and these were his words.

I never thought of writing a diary before. But this is the only way I can live on. This is my past that foreshadows my present. My guilt, my nostalgia. To be clear and precise, I'm starting from the very beginning of my life.

I was a baby when someone left me at the door of an orphanage. There they found me, and within no time I was a part of Little Angels. Grandma Mary named me Christopher, but my friends changed it by calling me Christoff. There everyone was happy, completely ignorant that they had at one time been deserted in their lives.

My friends were my life and there was this girl who I had a crush on. Her name was Charloette. We used to walk the backyard lawn together, climbing trees to catch a glimpse of the bird's nest, or even just strolling silently. We had a bond, but at that age I doubt one could call it love. Anyhow 7 years passed by like a whim, and we grew. She was very pretty, and kind, kind of like my best friend.

I remember it was one Sunday morning while we were playing in the lawn, when I saw Mary and two strangers watching us from the pier window. Ignoring their glances we continued our childlike stuff.

"You know Christoff, today's what day?" she said in her playful voice

"No, do you?"

"Today's friendship day, stupid,"

"Friendship. Yes I forgot. I brought a gift for you,"

"Really?"

"Yes close your eyes,"

She closed her eyes and I figgled into my pockets and said, "Now open them,"

In my hands was a locket that Mary and I had brought the previous day.

Her face turned happy and she smiled at me, "Thank you," she said.

"Open the locket," I told her.

And when she opened it she saw a picture of all the people of Little Angels.

"It's so beautiful," she said.

"Keep that with you,"

"Well I have a gift for you as well,"

She gave me a band with the quote, "Best friends forever,"

We both were jubilant and the day passed on merrily. It was when we were put to sleep, did the event occurred.

I was trying to sleep when I heard the door creak and found Mary at the door. She walked straight to me, and saw I was awake.

"Christopher, you're awake. It's good," she said.

"Yes Grandma, why are your eyes so watery?" I asked.

"My dear child," she said hugging me, "Charloette's gotta leave. The two people you saw today, want to adopt her,"

At this my heart went numb.

"Why does she have to leave?" I asked in a sad tone.

"Oh Christopher. See it like this. She's gonna get new parents who'll look after her, care for her. You wouldn't want to prevent her from this happiness,"

Sadly Grandma was right and with a heavy heart I said, "You're right. When does she leave?"

"This night," she said ,"I thought it be apt to tell you this since you two are best friends,"

Thereafter Mary walked me out to the outside gate, where she was standing with her new parents.

"They have adopted me," she said with a smile, "I'm leaving tonight, Christoff,"

"Yes, you are. I'm glad for you," I said putting up a happy face.

"Promise me, we'll be best friends even if I leave," she said.

"Yes. Best friends forever," I said as I shook her outstretched hand.

Thereafter she left in their car and I saw her waving me goodbye.

I stood there for some time before I turned and embraced Grandma and started crying.

"Grandma, she's happy. Then why am I not?"

"Christopher," she said looking at me in my eyes, "What you did for her is called sacrifice. And know this, it hurts to let go of someone you love and care for. But you did it for her happiness. And for that I am proud of you,"

That night I did sleep, but the memories didn't die away. A nostalgia forever gripped me in its fangs waiting for me to succumb to its grip. But I didn't 'cause I had a responsibility towards Mary and the children here.

Entangled Feelings

11 years later I found myself working at The Barrows. It was a good occupation. 5 hours work a day at the factory, and holidays on the weekend. The wages were good and altogether life was very much settled.

I shared quarters with a fellow associate and childhood friend named Jeffrey, and visited Grandma whenever I could. I was able to help her with the orphanage's financial part, and life went on like this for two years or so. But as philosopher's say, "Destiny's uncertain," and so it was when spring waltzed back again into my life.

It was a hard-working day. I was pretty much tired and was headed towards my apartment. Walking on the pavement in this bustling city, I often looked at the glass windows of the shops. And so it happened that I stood staring at a beautiful white wedding gown. For a few minutes I stared, and then I ostensibly looked at its price card.

"Phew! That's expensive," I remarked and walked on.

I was at the corner of the pavement, when I heard a voice calling out to me, "Christoff, Christoff , hold on,"

I turned round and noticed the unmistakable figure running towards me. For a moment I couldn't make out who it was until a lady stopped right in front of me breathing very hard.

Composing herself she said at last, "Damn, Christoff, you walk very fast,"

Clueless I stared before she noticed the blank expression on my face.

"You have forgotten me, haven't you?" she said haughtily.

"Uh…." I pondered at that curious angry look, "Who the hell is she? Stopping me in the middle of the pavement and acting all bossy. Did I ever know such a character?"

"Okay I'll give you a clue, you Alzheimer ridden BFF," she said sardonically.

"Alzheimer ridden BFF," I said offended.

"Wait a minute, BFF," I pondered as my tube light started blinking.

"You aren't Isabell, are you?" I asked expectantly.

"Yup dumbo. Who else could it be?" she said in her lively manner before embracing me.

"Thank God you recognized me Christoff, or else I'd end up slapping you for forgetting me so soon,"

As she let go I felt a warm flutter. Something that I had always longed for.

"Forgive me, it's been such a long time," I replied humbled.

"Yes that's true. This city seems new to me. Looks like I'll have a lot of catching up to do,"

"I'll help you with that,"

"I know you will. But let's get off the pavement first,"

"Yip."

I tried stopping a taxi but it just whisked past me as if I was invisible. Then I did the classic waving of my thumbs, but sadly that didn't work either.

"Your taxi hailing skills suck," taunted Isabell.

"Well you think you can do better?" I joustled back.

At this she gave a smile and whistled loudly at an ongoing taxi. The cab stopped right ahead and drove backwards towards us.

She made a winning glance at me as we stepped in and headed for the Prideaux Café.

"Foreign education taught you to whistle. That's impressive," I joked.

"It taught me a whole lot more than that. But what about you Christoff?" she said turning towards me.

"Well I'm employed and well off in my life,"

"Mary told me about your job and all that boring stuff of your life. What I meant is, are you seeing anyone?"

"Nope" I gave a quick reply.

"Still single," she laughed.

"Well that's a permanently temporary thing,"

"Let's hope so,"

As we alighted down, we noticed a surge of people at the Café.

"Looks like Miss Prideaux's business is running in top gear," said I.

"Hope she'll recognize us," replied Isabell.

The look of the Café had changed but its soul was still the same. Miss Julia Prideaux was never livelier than this as she commanded her subordinates with most enthusiasm.

"Come on girls, hasten up. Let's get this batch over it," she said in her Spanish accent.

"Gosh, there's no more seats," commented Isabell as we entered in, "You think she'll welcome us today?"

"Well let's ask her," I replied mirthful and walked to the counter.

"Any chance you'd treat two little children Julia," said I.

As she looked up her expression was one of surprise.

"Christopher," she exclaimed in a joyous tone, "Is that you?"

"Yup,"

At this Isabell advanced forwards greeting her, "Hi Julia,"

But sadly she couldn't recognize Isabell until I whispered in her ear some memorable details of her childhood.

"Tomboy looks with broken front teeth. You mean that Valentine girl," exclaimed Julia aloud.

On hearing that Isabell nudged her elbow onto my stomach side giving me some aching pain. And while she stared at me with that playful anger, Julia intervened.

"You two still haven't changed a bit," said she.

"I'd agree. She's still bossy like that tomboy,"

"Ignore him, Isabell," said Julia before embracing her, "You've grown into a beautiful lady,"

"Thank you," she replied in grace.

Miss Prideaux arranged for us two seats that had been kept reserved in the interior of the Café.

"Mam, the toppings are out," shouted a voice from the nearby kitchen.

"Coming," she answered.

"You two can sit here. I'll send Nancie shortly," she told us before leaving hurriedly.

Julia's a lively woman and a close friend of Mary's. Being kind hearted and jovial, whenever we'd visit her, she'd treat us with desserts, my favorite being the vanilla sundae.

"What's with that smile you're giving?" I asked curious.

"You're still wearing that locket," said he.

His observations had grown astute. And that evoked a rare compliment from me.

"I see that the Sherlock's spirit still hasn't left you, Christoff. As for the locket. It holds a memory I cherish,"

By now a pretty lady had joined in and was looking expectantly at us waiting for instructions.

"Nancie. Glad to see you're well," said Christoff.

"Well I can't thank you enough," she replied a bit flustered.

"Never mind Nancie. Meet Isabell. You know the girl I used to occasionally mention,"

At this a smile evidently overcame her expression as she said, "Nice meeting you Miss Isabell,"

"You're smiling. Is there anything wrong with me?" I asked puzzled.

"No, it's just that you're very different from what I expected you to be," said she.

"Different. How come?"

"You're very beautiful just the opposite of...."

"Well Nancie. I'd like to order...." Christoff barged in trying to change the topic. However I wasn't taking a dime of it. I put my hands on his mouth leaving him blabbering.

"Please continue Nancie,"

"You're not a bit tomboyish like Christoff used to tell me," she let it out at last.

"Uh huh. What else did he say about me?"

Nancie then looked at Christoff who was pleading her with his eyes to not answer my question. At this I placed my other hand on his eyes blocking his face shut.

Seeing my determined gaze, the innocent Nancie chose to answer. "Well he said you were very spunky with a moody tomboyishness just like Mowgli of the Jungle book,"

Christoff had wrestled my hands off his face and was now looking at Nancie giving her a helpless look. On the other hand my temper was about to explode.

"Well Nancie, today I'll show you my spunkiness," I said as I moved my legs under the roundtable before kicking the front rail of Christoff's chair backwards.

"Whoah," he shouted as he lost his balance and fell backwards before crashing against the wooden floor.

"That hurts," he said in agony.

Nancie helped him up before he sat, adjusting his chair quite a bit far from the table.

"Thank you Nancie for helping our Kipling up," said I in humour.

"Yup. I guess I'll need a coffee after this," replied Christoff.

"For you, Mam," said Nancie expectantly.

"Vanilla sundae," I answered.

As she left us, I gestured onto Christoff seeking his attention.

"Know what Christoff, I think Nancie here has a crush on you,"

"Nope. She's a sweet girl. She's just grateful for my help,"

"Help?" I asked curious.

"Now don't look at me like that,"

"Like what?"

"With that soul searching gaze, Isabell,"

"Okay… I won't delve further into this secret affair of yours," I teased him.

"Come on!"

"But there's something I need an honest answer to," I delved into the real topic.

"Go ahead,"

"Is there anyone who you love?" I asked staring into his eyes.

"Yes. I love you just like I love Mary, Isen…" he played innocent.

"Dumbass. Not that type of love. I mean the one where you get hitched up with her for your entire life,"

"Her. Entire life! You make it sound like a serious commitment,"

"It is. Particularly when I know who the girl is,"

"Don't be so conceited, Isabell,"

At this I gave a sigh and asked the inevitable

"Then why haven't you seen her for so long?"

"I didn't see you for the last five years. It doesn't mean that I was avoiding you," he said flippantly.

"No," I said in temper to his indifferent attitude, "Four years ago the feelings that you had for me turned into deep friendship which I consider…"

Christoff tried to reply but I was having none of this anymore.

"No, you listen. I know you've got your secrets. But Charloette is head over heels for you. She doesn't show it. But beneath that strong demeanour she seeks your embrace and love. So Christoff Myers upon my word, you will confess before her. Promise me,"

Christoff realized the change in my voice and finally opened up.

"I will. Just a little more time until the orphanage finds a new place. Then I'll be done,"

"I'll take that for now,"

For a short while I looked into Christoff's eyes.

"You dumbass. Stop looking at me so charmingly," I pondered as he gave that smile.

He has been like this ever since we were kids. Whenever anyone looked distressed he'd distract them with his lazy stupidity. And it worked to cheer us up. However when he was in a tight spot, he'd stay silent and give that smile as if putting up a pretence of "All is right,"

"You're still a buster," I said to him before Nancie re-entered the scene with a coffee and a Vanilla Sundae.

Now without any further ado, I took a big scoop and gobbled the delicious drooping vanilla. Christoff, meanwhile, maintained his suave manner and took light sips.

Friends' Day Out

It was on a Saturday, at 6 in the morning, did I receive a call from a dear friend.

"Yo! Christoff. How's work today?" spoke a jovial voice.

"You very well know that today's a holiday, Isen. And what's with you calling so early huh?" I said sardonically.

"O! My bad. But it's an important topic," he replied in humour.

"Important? Ok speak,"

"Nah it's not something to be discussed over phone. Can you meet me?"

"…Sure… I'm free,"

"Great, then meet me at the Charring Cross at 9," he said before cutting off the call.

"Well, he seems happy today," I pondered getting off bed.

Charring Cross lies in the countryside of Yorksville. It's a merry town, with a thriving economy, vast fields thronged with innumerable sycamores, and above all the only town that has a road leading towards the Hewlett valley. And so it was, that at quarter past seven I found myself seated on the westbound train headed towards Yorksville.

As the scenery of the distant urban areas faded into vast expanse of hills, and meadows, I kept observing the countryside through the windows.

"Beautiful," I pondered and relaxed into the tranquillity of the serene view.

By 9 I found myself at the intersection of the main town where I found Isen standing on the pavement searching for me.

"You look happy mate," I said greeting him.

"Glad you came on time,"

"So what's the important topic?"

He gave an unabashed smile and said it aloud, "Well today's the Beer Fest day in Charring Cross. And as such a great patron I am of drinking, I thought I'd need someone to carry me home at night,"

"Seriously! You brought me out on a holiday so that I can carry you off at night," I spoke in musing anger.

"Well I'll be drunk," he replied as in consolation to justify his request.

Since I had come this far from home, I might as well spend the day watching him get drunk.

"Alright….let's go Isen," I said complying.

"Now that's the Christoff I know," he laughed out loud.

The streets of Charring Cross lay gripped in festive fervour and mirth. Outside every shop hung the advert logo of Beer Fest while their vendors kept distributing leaflets to promote their stalls at the venue. However there was this one inn that stood out the most. Beside the street, right on the sidewalk round tables lay decorated in red silken cloth. Now most of us have seen those so called tricks involving pulling tablecloth without disturbing the utensils on it. It's a skilful art.

But have we seen the reverse. That is to say, let's just slip in the tablecloth beneath the invisibly thin glass over which the food plates, drinking cups brimmed up with latte rested without spilling a drop of it.

"Hey, you two dimwits. What are you staring at?" said an elegant voice.

"No way…It can't be you…Charloette," said I looking at the lady whose face lay hidden behind a fancy mask. As she removed it, a joyous smile greeted us both.

"Isen Hughes and Christoff Myers," she spoke delighted, "How on Earth did you two end up coming here?"

"Can't miss out on this Beer Fest, Charloette," spoke Isen in humour.

"You here, is understandable. But Myers, when did you become a drunkard?" she said looking keenly into my eyes.

"I heard you were serving free drinks. That's all," I joustled back.

"Really," There was a gleam in her eyes as she spoke.

"Actually he's here to carry me off," replied Isen.

At that remark she laughed at both of us and then encircling us by our shoulders, she ushered us in.

"Free drinks to all," she shouted aloud and everyone roared back in delight.

"How long has it been then, when the three of us were together?" spoke Charloette searching for something behind the counter.

"3 years. We last met at Mary's birthday," said I.

"Yeah…it was the summer of 1999," spoke Isen.

"Strange…ain't it? In teenage years we promised to see each other every now and then. But somehow we've gone separate ways," Charloette spoke handing Isen a Martini, and looking expectantly at me.

"Mango juice, Charloette," said I.

"He still refuses to drink," joked Isen.

"Old habits die hard," Charloette remarked as she searched for the bottle.

"Separate ways, you say. Not at all. I mean we're here together, aren't we? It's just like yesterday. Isen hasn't changed, nor have you,"

"And what about you Christoff?" she handed me the juice and looked straight at me.

"Well I work at the Barrows. Life's settled. What more can I expect?" I said with a smile.

"Your eyes speak otherwise. You know I visited Mary, a week earlier, she seemed worried about you,"

"Worried? Why? I'm all merry and happy,"

"Happy. Is it because Isabell's happy?" she finally held onto my weak nerve

"So that's why Mary hid it?" I spoke letting out a slight gasp, "That's just like her. But know what I'll find someone eventually,"

"That's like my bro," said Isen grabbing onto my neck as he messed up my hair.

A guy like him will love her with all his heart no matter what. Childhood love never dies. Especially when you end up being the best friend of that guy. It just gets suppressed with that humane logic, "If she's happy, then so am I," But the hurt comes and goes every now and then. And so was the case with Christoff. I won't deny that I love that guy. But I can't deny this either, I value his friendship more.

"So which place are you setting your stall at?" spoke Isen

"The third row front, beside the lakeside. And since you two are here I might save on the labour cost,"

"Whoops. She hasn't changed. Still bossy," whispered Christoff into Isen's ear.

"Yup…Looks like we have no choice,"

"Complain all you can, but both of you are helping me set up the tent and the decorations,"

"Yes definitely. Why won't we help?" fumbled Isen

"It seems you both have changed a bit. I didn't even need to pick my hockey stick this time," she mocked.

"Holy bejesus. Even the devil will look like a child before her," Christoff pondered.

Ultimately we spent much of that afternoon in setting up Charloette's stall. It took quite an effort but we finished it before evening.

Beer Fest

"You two aren't going to the Fest dressed like this, are you?" asked Charloette as we wrapped the jugs in the basket.

Isen and I both looked at each other trying to figure out what was wrong with our clothes.

"You idiots, you are going to get muddy, bloody soaked in water…It will be a literal brawl out here with drunk people dancing and partying till dawn. And mind you the lawmakers over here will look like puppets when that happens…." she spoke gutsily, "So you two better blend in with these country men, or you will be the first to get squashed,"

"Squashed?" asked Isen.

"You'll find out. But let's first get you some clothes," she said with a devilish smile on her lips.

So she took us to some local owner named Zico who gave us both board shorts and light t-shirts. After we came out dressed anew, he looked at us both, "Charloette, your friends will be the first today to get…."

"Squashed," she completed him, "I know,"

"I thought we were going to lakeside not to some beachside," complained Isen.

"Yeah these country people drink and party rowdier than any poolside party,"

It was 7 when we approached the lakeside but not before stopping by Charloette's lodgings.

"Give me 10 minutes," I'll be back she said ascending upstairs.

We both stood outside by the road as numerous people budged past us. And strangely all were wearing casual clothes.

"Bru, see that lady's... staring at us," said Isen pointing to a shack some yards away from us.

"Well its Beer Fest. Everyone's staring at everybody,"

As the clock struck ten minutes past seven, we heard light steps descending.

"I tell you mate. Charloette's not an ordinary girl. I mean she literally took ten minutes to get dressed up. That's some Guinness World record," said Isen amused.

However, a minute later all our amusement had turned into admiration. That is to say we were bedazzled. Dressed in a red wrapped mesh dress that draped down her flower-like ripped denim shorts, she smiled at us as her eyebrows evidently showed her amusement at our face's reaction. Messed up curls adorned her refreshingly resplendent face. But above all, it were those green eyes. They appealed to your soul.

"Let's roll out then," she spoke in her friendly manner.

"She's no ordinary girl. I tell you that, mate," Isen uttered as we walked behind her.

"Well, let's test it out,....You seem to have put on some weight," I shouted out to her.

"Really...When did you notice that?" she replied turning towards us.

"The moment I noticed the tattoo,"

"What tattoo?" she replied curious.

"Right along the midline, just above your waist, there's a tattoo. Made by a deft artist,"

"Impressive observation Christopher. What else can you make out?" she said in a challenging tone.

"I can't. I don't know the language," I gave a knowing smile at her.

"Χριστουφ, that's gibberish," complained Isen.

"Tough luck boys," she gave an enigmatic smile and walked away.

You see, people may call it Beer Fest but there's much more to this festival. Obviously the authorities don't allow children in here, but there's nothing too inappropriate either. As you can see there's the gigantic pool that is being set up. Shoot guns are being readied. Flashers are getting ready to showcase their reverse tablecloth tricks. Food stalls are peaking up their menus. To sum it up, its chaotically enthusiastic over here.

As night fell over, the lakeside got flooded with teenagers, and tourists. The security officials were having a tough time dealing with such a huge crowd. But all in one, the party was about to kick-start. With the ceremonious church bell ringing exactly at 8, a huge roar erupted into the sky. No sooner one could see tomatoes flying high and low, hitting people's faces as a cherry red colour inundated the pool side.

"Newbies," shouted out some locals as they saw us enter the lakeside.

"What? No wait, I'm a born countrysider," Isen tried bluffing. But those people weren't listening.

"Whoah," we shouted in unison as they carried us off our feet.

"Good luck boys," Charloette spoke bidding adieu.

"Bru, I don't have a good feeling about this," said Isen in a desperate voice.

"Neither do I,"

Those mob tied each of us to roundtable tops whose rim were aligned vertically onto a circular track that kept spiralling outwards and broke off tangentially at diametrically opposite points straight towards the lake.

"Squash time, people," roared a heavy voice. And no sooner tomatoes came flying at us. Whack after whack we kept getting hit.

"Fools. Start rolling," shouted Charloette from vicinity.

"Alright. Isen go clockwise. I'll go the other way,"

"What?" he said dazed.

"Spiral outwards. That's all,"

"But the lake,"

"It's either whacking tomatoes or the lake,"

"Lake. Definitely the lake,"

"Ok now," I screamed aloud

Sadly our first attempt wasn't synchronized and we just ended up missing our tangential outbreaks ultimately hitting each other. Our minds were rolling nuts and the squashing tomatoes that were being hurled at us kept us all the more energized.

"Ok Isen... Use your wrists. Go clockwise and make sure you take the exit going in the same direction,"

"Wait you mean the second one,"

"Yup, just get rolling,"

A few seconds later I too got into my act. Isen had gotten out of the first circle. Now it was my turn.

"Now. Sync it Myers," I pondered on and on. And out I went into the second spiral.

"Whew. First circle's gone,"

"Know what Christoff, these people are taking us, urban citizens' chivalry for granted," Isen shouted.

"Yes. Let's just grab onto to those red fruits and hurl them back onto their faces,"

"Yup. Counter attack mate,"

We did as planned. We rolled, got squashed a few times, managed to pick some tomatoes and hurled it back into the encircling crowd.

Some of the dimwits with slow reactions got stunned at our fight back and cheered us on.

"Your friends are crazy, Charloette," said Zico.

"Yes they are. That's why they are my friends," replied Charloette with appreciation, "You two, let's get this over with," She cheered us on.

"Ok Isen let's just repeat what we did," said I.

"Yup,"

We two did exactly as earlier, got ourselves our two exits but this time we rolled out as wheels straight up the wooden slope.

"Awwww. I'm going to die..." screamed Isen in mid-air.

"Mate try to land on your back," I shouted up the parabolic path before we both came crashing down.

"Brace yourself for impact," said Isen in freaking humour.

"This ain't no Titanic movie, Isennnnn…" I joustled back and bang we hit the waters as it splashed straight onto the onlookers drenching them wet. And as for us we were alive.

"Whoah…So that's squashing. Baby I love it," said Isen aloud.

"You love it. A minute earlier you were fubaring your life out,"

After locals freed us off our knots, we swam back to land again, where Charloette greeted us with her charming smile.

"Really, you two are nuts," she said taking us by our shoulders, "Ten minutes, that's the fastest one has ever gotten out of squashing. And to top that you hurled back tomatoes at them. By the way whose idea was that?"

"Christoff's," said Isen shaking my hand, "Mate I owe you one today," He was still trying to catch breath as Charloette dredged us to her stall. But as we stood there, the night breeze whisking past our wet dress made us shiver.

"It's a good thing that I brought these," said Charloette handing us our usual clothes,"

"Yeah, the new ones didn't last even for fifteen minutes," joked Isen.

"Squashing does that. Now get into the racks and change them," she said as a customer joined us, "And be quick,"

"Yes mam," we both said in unison and left.

Dressed in our usual attire we sat there, encircled by drunkards with beer jugs flying high. Charloette cooked us some warm spaghetti noodles and accompanied with marshmallows, they soothed down our nerves, at least temporarily.

That is to say, after four jugs of simmering brandy we lost our buddy Isen to absolute sobriety.

"Ah there he goes," said I as Isen delved into the sea of drunkards.

At this Charloette gave a slight smile and said, "He won't change. But what about you Christoff, I heard you are still working at the Barrows,"

"Well they pay well, and the job's a decent one,"

"Still… repairing broken bikes and cars, that wasn't your forte. You were adventurous, kind of like the guy who'd be in the police nabbing criminals,"

That caught me by surprise for a moment.

"…Well… you're right. I had even applied… but they found me too spirited for on field work. So here I am repairing… broken police vehicles and what not in that fancy impound of theirs,"

At this she gave a sigh and after a slight shake of her head spoke

"You still can't lie, can you?"

That moment, when those green eyes stared straight into my soul, I felt nervous.

"It's okay Christoff. If you don't want to tell me, I won't press you. But don't lie to me…"

"Lie?" I played innocent.

At this she gave a knowing smile and then answered in a solemn tone.

"I went to the Barrows to meet you. There I found Jeffrey and he acted very weird. It's as if as he was hiding something. Eventually I left, but my suspicion always lingered on,"

"No, no…he must have been worried that if some higher official saw you, we might get into trouble for slacking off at work,"

"Either way Christoff, just don't get yourself into trouble,"

"I won't."

As I sat there listless, Charloette left to attend to her customers. With people partying the night out, I won't deny that I found myself alone sitting on a wooden tool and gazing at the surging crowd of merry people. That was my life in a nutshell. Tragic loneliness.

A few minutes later I would have even dozed off, had I not seen Isen being dredged in by a lady.

"He's lost it," said Charloette joining in.

But before I could reply Isen barged in introducing the newfound friend of his.

"Bru, meet Scarlett. Scarlett, these are my friends, Christoff and Charl….,"

He was so drunk that even before he could introduce us properly, he fell onto the ground asleep.

"So much for Beer Fest, he fell asleep even before midnight," I replied and got him up a chair.

"Thank you for bringing him here," I told the lady.

"Never mind. I just remembered seeing you two together at the Squash. When I found him so much inebriated I brought him here," replied the lady.

"Well… that was nice of you Miss…"

Somehow I had forgotten her name.

"…Joyce. Joyce Scarlett. That's my name," she said offering me her hand.

"I am Christoff Myers," I said reciprocating the gesture, "And she's my friend Charloette Whitman,"

"Charloette," she said in a cheerful voice, "It's nice to have finally met you. People here admire you a lot for standing up against Diego's brother,"

"Who's Diego?" I asked looking at Charloette.

"Well he's the drug lord who runs this town," replied Joyce.

"Jeese…Charloette, you went up against that Mafia's brother," I asked in a solemn tone.

"Not much to worry about. His henchmen were nagging me to close the Inn. Then one day when I didn't relent, they tried to use force. And when that happened you know the consequences, Christoff,"

"You just don't beat criminals like that. You could have reported to the police,"

"Didn't you hear what she said? His brother owns this town,"

"She's right. The law officials here are just his puppets" said Joyce

"Either way, that doesn't justify the use of your hockey stick. Remember this, brave deeds no matter how courageous they may be, often bring fatal consequences, Charloette. Be careful,"

"Okay," said Charloette, "Relax. It's fest time. Let's not delve into these topics,"

"Yeah. She's right. It's party time and I was wondering if you two could join us for the dance at the Gala," said Joyce in an expectant voice.

"Dance and he. That'd be interesting" said Charloette teasing me.

"Well I can dance a bit," I replied to the challenge.

"So why don't you two come?"

"Nah…You can count me out. I've got this stall to look after. But do take Christoff. It'll be interesting to see those crazy dance moves he's gonna invent,"

That mystical laugh of hers piqued me a bit.

"Okay, Joyce let's go," I said at last.

The Reaper's Wrath

"Where did Christoff go?" asked a drowsy Isen.

"He went dancing with Joyce" said I.

"So her name's Joyc…" muttered Isen before whiting out again.

"Crazy fellow" said Zico who had just joined in with little Alicia.

"You know you aren't supposed to bring children here,"

"Well, I had to set up my stall and since Alicia's mother out of town today, she's tagged along with me,"

"Here Alicia, take this," I said handing over the candy.

"Thank you," said the little girl.

"She's very cute,"

"Yup…she's gone after her mother," replied Zico.

"Mam, a Bloody Rose over here please," shouted a customer.

"Mam!" smiled Zico.

"Yip. They know the punishment for misbehaviour," I said pointing towards the hockey stick.

"Yeah that's pretty severe,"

As I looked down the counter for the drink I realized I had run out of it.

"We've run out of Rose, mister" said I.

"Well if you have any stock tucked in somewhere, me and my friends are willing to wait," he replied mirthful.

"Okay, just wait for fifteen minutes, I'll go and bring the remainder of the bottles,"

"You're going to the Inn?" asked Zico.

"Yeah. Just look after the stall for a while until I return,"

"Sure, I will,"

The inn was hardly a block away and the alleyways would cut short the distance even more. So within ten minutes I found myself near the Inn. After getting the requisite bottles I hurried down the same path towards the Fest.

"I see you're awake again, Isen"

"Zico, now where did Charloette go?"

"To the Inn. She'll be back anytime now,"

Just as Zico uttered those words his friend Moretz came rushing in.

"Catch your breath buddy,"

"That Vega....Alejandro Vega and his men...I saw them at the outskirts of the town,"

"Vega. What's he doing here?"

"Who's Vega?" asked Isen now completely alert.

"The gangster's brother whose men Charloette beat up the other day,"

"Then he spells trouble. And to top that Charloette still hasn't returned," Isen said worried.

"Yeah, gather all the officials and let's head out towards the Inn," Zico told Moretz.

I took a right turn into an alleyway heading towards the Fest.

"Ten more minutes and I should be there," I pondered.

Just as I emerged out of the narrow corridor, a jeep whisked past so close to me that I lost my balance and the glass bottles in the crate came crashing down.

"Assholes," I shouted in its direction and just then a man sitting at the back of that jeep glared at me. He gave a devilish smile and shouted out to his mates

"We've found her"

Right at that moment the driver turned the jeep around and headed back towards me.

As it drove closer I could make out two faces. And those were the people I had beaten the other day.

I couldn't run for when I sensed the danger it was already too late.

Five men descended down and each of them were holding a hockey stick.

Their leader clearly stood out from the rest of his goons and spoke in clear threatening voice.

"We've come to return the favour,"

"So you're just gonna attack on a defenceless lady. That's really cheap," I said unafraid.

"I told you she's cocky," said a henchmen.

"You know what I like about ladies like you?" Vega asked taunting me.

"I ain't no lady that you've met so far, you dumbass,"

At this he whistled and clapped his hands.

"Good. I admire you for your courage, lady," he mocked "So know what, I'll give you a fighting chance,"

He then threw his hockey stick towards me and said, "Pick it up and fight,"

I did as he asked and now with a confidence in my voice I said aloud, "You'll regret this. 'Cause I'm gonna beat you down to a pulp"

All the four goons attacked me at once. But to be honest they were amateurs. With the wild swings they all took it gave me ample time to countcrattack.

I sidestepped the vertical blow from the right and with a short jab of my elbow, I broke his lower jaw. Then with the other end of my stick blocking the left downward swing I swung the heavy end right to his temple. As for the third goon who tried swinging towards my lateral side onto the ribs, a high kick to his nose fended off his attack. The final one, however, was a bit clever. He tried landing a kick onto my stomach which I backed away from and then with a right swing I knocked his senses out.

Finally the boss remained. I walked towards him and put the stick straight at his neck.

"Any final wishes?" I asked.

"Feisty. And I love it," he smeared at me.

"That's enough," I said and began to take a swing.

But just at that moment a click followed with the weight of a pistol's nape pressed against the back of my head.

"Game's over, Senorita," said Vega brushing aside the stick and then wrestling it off my grip.

One of his men had sneaked up behind my back and was pointing a gun behind my head.

"Get her into the alleyway and you two, guard the opposite entrances," Vega ordered his men, "And if anyone tries to enter in, shoot him."

They dragged me by my wrists into the corridor and his men kept guard.

"What's going on?" Christoff asked Isen as he entered into the Gala seeming very worried.

"Vega's brother and his men have entered Charring Cross and they're after Charloette," he shouted aloud trying to overcome the music. However, he wasn't very audible.

So they left the lakeside and made their way towards a much quieter vicinity.

"What about Charloette?" Christoff asked.

"Damn it, Christoff. Vega's brother and his men are after Charloette. Zico's friend saw them heading towards the Inn,"

Those words snapped him out of the doldrums.

"Where's Charloette now?" he asked anxious.

Isen didn't have an answer.

"Isen, can't you hear me? Where's Charloette?" his voice seemed distressed.

"She went towards her Inn but hasn't returned," he replied, "Zico and the officials are already out there searching for her."

"Well then, let's go there"

They both hastily made their way out of the Fest and were en-route towards the Inn.

Ten minutes is all it took when they found themselves on the streets running westwards until a mob, gathered outside an alleyway, caught their attention.

The henchmen pinned me onto the wooden utility pole as Vega instructed them to.

"Hey there, what are you all doing?" shouted a voice outside the alleyway.

"Looks like the Sheriff, boss" said the guarding henchmen towards the right.

"Just when we needed him," smiled Vega.

"You, go there and get his cuffs," he ordered one of his men.

He let go of me while the other kept his grip firm on my wrists.

"Hey there Sheriff. Boss needs your cuffs,"

"But the lady…." retaliated the Sheriff.

"You just worry about your family, Sheriff. I heard your daughter's grown into a very beautiful woman. Now you wouldn't want any harm to befall her now, would you?" the goon taunted the powerless man.

"That's better. Hand me those cuffs and keep silent. We'll get through this together if you continue being a nice puppy like this," he laughed as the Sheriff handed him the cuffs.

"Well done," Vega told his man as he brought him the cuffs.

"Tie her hands high up. Yeah just like that. Now cuff her wrists there," Vega ordered as they pinned me onto the pole.

"You're the feistiest woman I've met so far," he said as he grabbed onto my neck.

"And know this all of the twelve woman who were in this position screamed relentlessly as I violated them" he said staring into my eyes before he kissed me on the lips.

His stench was abominable and before he could respond I kicked him hard on his balls with my thigh.

"I guess you must have gotten kicked down there a lot. Must be painful when you can't have kids anymore," I answered gutsily as he backed off in pain and agony.

"You bitch. Just wait till I teach you a lesson," he cursed.

"That's it. You two go to the entrances and keep watch along with them. I'll handle this women now," he spoke in temper.

He then grappled onto my shoulders and tried to force himself on me. In that tussle he slapped me on the face and kept groping me as those scratches began to bleed.

"She's in there. They've got both the entrances covered, and they're armed," said Zico as we approached the alleyway.

"Sheriff, you've got to stop them," Christoff pleaded.

"I can't son. He owns this town. No one can go up against him," replied a broken voice.

"That's bullshit. You've got the goddarn police force behind you. And they're just gonna stand and watch. Why?" Isen revolted in a conflicted voice.

"Coz we're only as strong as Alejandro de la Vega wants us to be,"

At this a crazy frenzied violence fell over Christoff and for the first time in his life Isen witnessed his buddy's real identity.

"So you won't help. Then I assume you won't stop me either," Christoff spoke in a grave voice.

"Stop you from what?" asked the Sheriff.

But Christoff was already off as he picked up the hockey stick just as Charloette's scream started echoing in the vicinity.

The pain was agonizing and I started screaming as blood began to drip onto the road. Yet he kept fondling until he tore off my dress. But he didn't stop there. Suddenly he turned me against the pole and kept me pinned there as he tried to strip down my pants.

For a moment he kind of stopped and then said, "I see you've got a tattoo on your waist. Ah it's Greek…"

"Χριστουφ. That's the guy's name, huh. Too bad he isn't here," he laughed aloud.

Those words remembered me of him. And I just wished he would somehow come here to end this nightmare.

The officials gave way as Christoff advanced. His eyes were blood red with anger. And his oncoming wrath was about to unleash.

The first henchmen guarding the right entrance had slacked off expecting no resistance.

His gun was still in his right hand when he saw Christoff approaching him.

"Back off….." he tried threatening.

But by the time he could put his finger on the trigger, Christoff had dashed forward and then having grabbed his hand with the stick's scoop, he twisted it right, sending the gun off in mid-air.

The gunshot echoed into the vicinity. But this was just the beginning.

A left high kick to the temple knocked the man over as the gun fell back into Christoff's left arm. In that split moment before anyone could react he fired a shot at the second goon's palm. His maimed fingers let go of the gun and soon he found his neck in that scoop of the hockey's stick as Christoff pulled him downwards straight onto his knee that went right up the goon's chin, battering down any life in him.

The remaining two henchmen had come forward to protect their boss. But that proved to be a fatal mistake.

"You bastard, you think you can just walk in and kill us all," said one of the goons.

"Enough talk," said Christoff as he fired two bullets. One that crippled the blabbering man shut. The other which pierced the shooting shoulder of the last henchman.

Then in no time the stick's heel punched through one's stomach while the other received a fatal swirling kick to his right neck. As the final henchman tried to recuperate from that punch, a backward blow onto his head from the stick's shaft, knocked him out cold.

As the battle noise died down, an eerie silence fell over. Then slowly the thumping of one's steps approached Vega.

"Don't come forward," said a frightened Vega as he tried putting a gun onto Charloette's head. But he was too slow. Before he could bend his elbow, a bullet seared into his left arm making it senseless.

"Curse you," screamed Vega as the gun slipped through his bleeding fingers.

As the walking man's figure emerged from the silhouette, Charloette looked in his direction.

"Christoff," she whispered out as tears started rolling down those injured cheeks.

Seeing her friend cuffed to the pole in that pitiable crying state, Christoff couldn't tolerate the indignity that she had suffered at the hands of her molester.

His expression said it all, and the object of his wrath was standing right in front of him.

He let go of the pistol and lashed out at Vega with such tremendous force that the hockey stick's head splintered after the impact on his left temple.

A kick straight at the ribs followed by a jaw-breaking punch knocked Vega out. But Christoff wasn't relenting.

As Vega lay pinned on the ground, Christoff kept smashing his bloodied face till it was barely recognizable. One more punch and he'd be dead.

As he lifted his fist one more time, Charloette's voice stopped him.

"Don't do it Christoff. Please stop," she cried out.

"But he tried to… He tried to rape you," he shouted conflicted.

"And you've given him the punishment. Anymore and he would die," she pleaded.

"He deserves it," he retaliated and lifted his arm.

"May be he does. But I can't see my friend become a murderer just to avenge me. Please, let go of him Christoff," her voice broke into a sob, "Please do it if you love me."

Those words halted Christoff midway before he let go of all his anguish by punching the road besides Vega's face.

As his anger faded, he got up and walked back towards Charloette. There, after picking up the gun he fired a shot breaking those cuffs off.

Shaken as Charloette was by the deafening sound, Christoff removed his jacket slipping it around her shoulders. Then with a sad smile he looked at those teary eyes before clasping her head onto his shoulders.

"You stubborn girl," he said kissing her on the forehead, "It's okay to cry when you're hurt."

Those words comforted her and so she let go crying bitterly.

Heart Strings

There's something deeply ingrained in humans. No matter how strong we may be, someday life will humble us out. One just hopes on that particular day you've got those friends who'll stick their necks out for you and help you stand back up.

And indeed he was one such friend.

By 4 we found ourselves seated in the train heading back Riviera. Charloette had received the initial treatment but staying at Charring Cross wasn't a wise choice, especially when you make enmity with the drug lord who runs that town.

Christoff sat opposite to me with Charloette's head resting on his shoulder. She was awake staring fixatedly at those marks. Probably those harrowing memories wouldn't let her sleep. Christoff, on the other hand, was lost in deep thought as he gazed through the window.

We sat silent for a while. But all of us were restless. So many things had happened in that span of a night that our humane logic still found it difficult to put those pieces together.

"Christoff," said Charloette.

"Yes, what happened?" he asked in a caring tone.

"Can you sing me the lullaby that Mary used to when she put us to sleep?"

"Sure," he replied and sang in a hopeful voice.

"Hold on to those feelings
that make you so true.
Always remember those laughs
that crackled inside you.

Staying true to yourself
dance through a rainy day.

And when the night falls
you star-up each other's sky.

'Coz inside each of you
flutters a Little Angel.
Blossoming up Someone's life
with love and mirth.

Always remember these heart strings
that bridge our lives.
For at their ends we'll stand
waiting for you with open arms."

By the time Christoff finished, Charloette had dozed off onto his shoulders.

"Isen," he spoke in a careful whisper.

"If Jeff calls, answer it for me" he said handing me his cell phone.

After a while, when I went to the washroom to splash some much needed water onto my dreary eyes, did Christoff's cell start vibrating in my pocket.

I picked it up and answered

"Jeff, it's Isen,"

"Isen…where's Christoff?" he inquired.

"He's with Charloette. He didn't want any disturbance. Hence he told me to relay the information you gave,"

"Okay. Tell him I ran a background check on Vega. Apparently Alejandro de La Vega is guilty of raping twelve innocent women in the Reut rape rally, murdering the head priest of The Viet, smuggling drugs across the Naome. The list goes on mate. Can't say he's done any wrong by beating him to a pulp," said Jeffrey.

"We're lucky Christoff's rage didn't kill anyone," said I.

"Yeah Isen. The Reaper's rage is quite something. But according to our ground team's report, they are all crippled for the rest of their lives"

"That means only one thing. Vega's elder brother will come after him for sure,"

"Don't worry about Alex. He's already on our list. He'll be taken care of,"

"So you guys work in some sort of secret agency?"

"Nah. I'll let Christoff explain it to you. We'll be at the station at seven, buddy," he replied before ending the call.

Prelude To Winter

"You owe us an explanation, Christoff," asked Isen as I joined in.

"I do?" I replied innocent.

"Yes, you do" retorted Charloette.

"About what?"

"Don't go around fooling us, you smart alec. Isen told me how you beat those rascals," she said angrily.

"I was angry that's all," I tried playing it down.

"Yeah, the Reaper's anger is quite something," Isen said lifting his eyebrows.

"Jeff?" I inquired giving a wry smile.

"Yipp,"

"Look Christoff, you can either tell us now or we'll do it before Mary," scolded Charloette staring sharply with those killer green eyes.

"Fine. No need to use her to blackmail me," I gave in at last.

"Before I begin I need you to promise me something," I finally got serious.

"Go on,"

"First. Mary and everyone else you know, will be kept out of this. Second. You will stay at the Barrows in Riviera until I deal with Vega,"

"You can't be serious," Charloette revolted.

"I am,"

"I won't let you risk your life for me," she raised her voice.

"The fight is inevitable. Diego de La Vega will come after you to get to me. We have gotten a head start. So that'll play well to our advantage,"

"But Jeff said that your agency will take care of him. They have even sent a ground team there," said Isen.

"Paradox Code, Isen. The ground team is Diego's men. We'll take care, in our language means one thing. He's coming after you. Fend for yourself,"

"Crap,"

"Ok with the conditions out, here's the real deal."

The Barrows is a legally non-existent entity that works directly with the top echelons that run every country. We're their fail-proof system. Any extradition that will meet long-term jurisdiction and legal frailties are our assignment. We are the by-pass, the unofficial aid that every government knows about and when needed will make use of. If caught during extraditing a target, our agents are disavowed and the organization kept an open secret,"

"That's some 007 stuff," replied an astounded Isen.

"Yeah. And as a disguise we work under the police's impound repairing junk,"

"It's a risky job hunting foreign criminals," commented Charloette.

"Yes, but don't worry about me. It's been two years since I joined this field. And I haven't gotten shot at even once," I assured her.

"One more thing," said Isen, "Why do they call you Reaper?"

"You have to ask Jeff about that and looks like he's right on time," Christoff said as we reached Riviera station.

As we alighted down Jeffrey and four other people greeted us in an impromptu manner.

"Your agency isn't very professional," I remarked.

"Trust me Charloette. We are the best when it comes to extradition," replied Jeffrey.

"Their attire seem otherwise,"

"Ah these people. I just hired them to drive the cabs along the way,"

"Four taxis. One for each. Splendid," Isen said amused.

"There are birds watching us right," commented Christoff.

"Yes. Diego put a bounty on Charloette, and pretty much anyone who's seen with her," said Jeffrey.

"That's bad news," said a timid Isen.

"Actually it's good. Let's move," Christoff gave a brisk reply and we started heading for the entrance.

"Jeff. Mary and the orphanage. You've got them covered?" asked Christoff.

"Yes,"

"Great. Now, Charloette and Isen as we enter outside you'll see four taxis. Select each for yourself and get seated"

"Whoa, we split so they can't trace us easily," said Isen

At this Christoff gave a devilish smile before we entered into our respective taxis.

"Boss, the four of them have taken separate cabs," said a henchman.

"Get your men to follow them. They're playing decoy with us. But we'll catch them all," said a vengeful voice.

"Yes," replied the goon as he carried out his instructions.

"No matter how many cabs you all take, you can't outnumber the bounty hunters chasing you,"

The four cabs diverged at the intersection as expected but they all made a fatal mistake. They went into the lonely downtown areas. And that made it simpler.

As the cab entered into the lonely side road the goons surrounded it bringing it to a stop. The driver surrendered before the guns. Now, only one thing remained.

A henchman walked out and opened the car's door. However, all he found was a large circular hole carved right at the bottom, with a written note stuck at the backseat.

His cell started ringing and just like him, his co-workers had found an empty car with a note containing the same number.

"Everyone's here," inquired Christoff as Isen, Jeffrey and I made our way into the car.

"Yeah," I replied.

"Great. Let's roll out," he said gearing down the black SUV.

"That's some insane stuff you pulled out there," said Isen laughing.

"It's quite simple Isen," Christoff replied.

"Yeah, he called me at night and instructed me to bring these cabs. Specially designed in our tech-yard with black glasses and a hole if you recognized it. We specifically parked these above the open manhole through which you just climbed down," explained Jeffrey.

"And your co-workers covered it up after we had descended," I said impressed.

"Exactly,"

"So this is your job Christoff," I remarked.

"Yup. But it's just begun," he said in a focused tone and continued driving.

It took an hour to reach the dilapidated building which overshadowed the Barrows true identity. And no sooner did we enter in than we were greeted with curious gazes as all the people scrutinized us. Isen and I stood there evidently nervous, before Jeffrey and Christoff walked in behind us.

"Don't just stand there. Follow me," said Christoff as he hurriedly took a turn into the right corridor.

As he uttered those words all the people instantly resumed their work and we quickly followed in Christoff's footsteps straight into his office.

"Jeff, dig up the data about Greenwich bombing," said Christoff as he stood at the glass window surveying the streets.

As instructed Jeffrey dabbled at his laptop and quickly replied

"Yuvisko Helinsky, an expert in time and remote detonating explosives, was charged with mass murder for the Greenwich bombing. His current whereabouts are unknown but he's wanted for treason and espionage against the Greats,"

"He was at the station. I remember his face,"

"Well, he's not the type to go after bounties,"

"No. He must work for Diego. And that means only one thing Jeff,"

"Diego plotted the massacre,"

"Yup and he's coming after us,"

That discussion told us about the gravity of the danger that loomed before us. And for a moment I thought that I was to blame for this situation.

Christoff probably recognized this and said, "I'll close this matter, Charloette. No one will be harmed. That's my word to you,"

"How do you intend to do that?" asked Isen.

"When a snake's injured, it'll bite anything that comes after it. I'm gonna use this animal tendency of humans,"

"You'll go after him alone, won't you?" inquired Jeffrey.

"Yipp. And looks like he's taken the bait," said Christoff as the office telephone started ringing.

"You were foolish to leave your number" said a deadly voice.

"I'd say we skip the formalities Diego. Your brother's taken my greeting. So let's just get to the point," replied a cold Christoff.

"The point is that you think you have it all under your control. But let me warn you. The pain that is about to be inflicted on you is going to be unfathomable,"

"You are good at bragging. However I propose we meet and settle this once and for all,"

"Meet you say. What makes you believe that I'll let you walk out alive?"

"Because I have what you don't and you have what I need. An exchange. That's all,"

"The papers. So you've got it. That would make a trade feasible. But what is it that you want from me?"

"Two things. But I'll tell that when we meet,"

"Very well then. Come to Hogan Factory at 5 today. And I hope you know the laws out here,"

"Sure do. It'll be quite a spectacle," Christoff smiled enigmatically putting down the receiver.

"What papers were you talking about?" asked Charloette.

"The ones I got from his brother. It has the details of all his cash houses in this country. The names of his partners, the loopholes through which his money is siphoned, pretty much everything to nail him down,"

"Then hand it over to the police. They'll catch him," said Isen.

"Yep. They'll arrest them right at the Hogan factory. That's easy," Jeff joined in.

"No. It has to be me,"

"Why? He'll kill you the moment you hand him the papers," revolted Charloette.

"He won't. Have faith in me. This is way beyond vengeance for what I did to his brother. I'll just have to find out the reason though. For that I'll have to meet Diego."

And with that, Christoff left the Barrows for the factory paying no heed to our concerns.

Hogan was located on the outskirts of Riviera. It used to manufacture shipping equipment but had been abandoned for a decade after an oil spillage at Cue Coast destroyed all marine life. That is to say without leverage my escape stood no chance.

I pulled over by the roadside and there it stood.

With the setting sun casting a looming silhouette over the front, I took a deep breath recalling the events that led me to this place. And to be honest this was certainly the biggest puzzle of my life.

I entered in as dusk enshrouded the vicinity. Pitch darkness with streams of moonlight trickling through broken tinged windows decorated this place of gloom. A cold wind rushed in behind my neck alerting my heightened senses. I stopped calming my frayed nerves.

And as soon as I took a step forward, a laser beamed straight onto my forehead.

"You know you are either the cleverest person or the biggest fool I have met so far," a voice hissed surreptitiously.

"Still hiding your identity," I replied unfazed, "Or should I say... Scarlett,"

"Marvellous," clapped Joyce emerging from the shadows into the moonlight. Her crimson eyes were gleaming and her enigmatic smile said it all.

"You're worthy of that title, Christoff," she said advancing towards me.

"An impressive façade, Scarlett. Entire world after a man, while a woman roams around in plain sight pulling strings from the shadows. But that's expected of the mastermind behind the Greenwich massacre,"

"I give it to you," she stood before me, "I honestly didn't think that the guy I danced with last night would turn out to be the Reaper,"

"You missed the perfect chance to kill. And so did I. But that's in the past. The present is what concerns me,"

She stood motionless weighing in my words.

"So what gave me away?"

"Your curiosity. Distracting me away from Charloette and digging up information on me from Isen. That's what a poacher does,"

Her crimson eyes stared fervently at mine as she inched closer and with a bated breath kissed me.

"I couldn't resist," she said as she withdrew, "You're the first one to have outdone me. That's why you'll live."

The laser on my forehead went out. The thump of one's foot echoed into my ears as my eyes stared expectantly towards the figure that emerged behind Joyce's shoulder.

It was my best friend Isabell who was holding the gun.

"Surprised," whispered Joyce into my ear, "And just so you know, she volunteered,"

"Volunteered. That's your subtle way of coercing people to obey you,"

"It's your loss Christoff. Now hand me the papers,"

I didn't care to answer her. Isabell's eyes were pleading for me to comply.

"The papers, Christoff," demanded Scarlett impertinently.

"A captive," I spoke in a clear voice to my friend before handing over my leverage to Joyce.

"See. This is your weakness Christoff. Your friends. I knew it the moment I met you at Charring Cross. That's the reason why I took Isabell's husband as a hostage,"

Christoff remained silent as if he was waiting for something to happen. And it wouldn't be any later before that opportune moment finally arrived.

The silence that loomed so eerily in this air of solitude was broken by the ring of a cell phone. It was Joyce's.

Her expression changed in an instant when a gunshot blasted out over the cell and her henchmen were heard scurrying for help saying, "It's a trap. We are surrounded,"

"How did you…," For the first time I saw fear in Scarlett's eyes and a tremble was evident in her hand as the cell slipped onto the ground.

"You're wrong. They aren't my weakness. My friends are my strength. Otherwise, who in their right mind would risk their lives being held as a hostage just to lead us to your hideout. As long as you held Hosse captive, Isabell here remained your puppet. But that string has now been cut,"

said Christoff audaciously.

And just like that the tables had turned.

Isabell pointed the nape of the gun on Joyce's head.

"As soon as your lover goes free, you'd mutiny against me," Joyce scorned.

"You have been outplayed. Accept your defeat," said Isabell with renewed confidence.

"So, it seems for now," Joyce conceded clenching her teeth in vengeful sprite.

Later, officials from the Barrows arrived at Hogan to take Joyce away to the penitentiary where she would probably spend the rest of her life.

A Piper's Kiss

"Well, why don't we play together?"

"Yeah that would be nicer than brooding here alone," Isen joined in.

"Doesn't it bother you that Isabell is gone?" I replied morose.

"Well it does. But do you remember how we used to quarrel as to who would get to marry her?"

"Yeah and one day we asked her opinion on this?"

"She chose me,"

"Really. I can't seem to remember why,"

"Because I am taller than you Christoff" Hosse jabbed at me,"

"So much for judging a man's worth by his height," I complained.

"You see Christoff, we'll keep in touch with her. I'm pretty sure one day we'll have all these tiny communication devices to talk our hearts out with each other in the future,"

"Well at least I now know that your flirting will go digital for sure. May be right across to random girls on different continents at the same time,"

"Flirting and me. I am a straight chap Chris. When I see a pretty girl, I tell her she's beautiful. Unlike you who holds onto to feelings without confessing,"

"Feelings and me. Aren't you the same age as me to give advice on relationships?"

"But I'm not stupid,"

"And I am?"

"Yes. Otherwise who in their sound mind, can't see that there's a girl who's head over heels for you. And every time you seem sad, she becomes morose,"

"And who is she?" I asked dimwittedly.

"See Isen. Everyone here knows except our Sherlock, "Hosse said flustered.

"Is it that obvious?" I asked earnestly.

"It's like the Moses 12th commandment you Einstein. Charloette likes you,"

"Your sister likes me?" I said surprised.

"Yes you tube light. Now will you go and talk to her. It will cheer her up,"

"But she always acts so spunky and bossy. Until now I only thought of her as a friend. But this changes everything. I can't talk casually to her again knowing she likes me,"

"You're overthinking it buddy," said Isen aptly.

"Ok. Because you're my friend and it's my sister who's involved, I'll tell you this. She usually does not like to be complemented unless it's from me. And seeing she likes you, I suggest you do the same,"

"So I tell her she looks pretty when she orders us around with that hockey stick of hers. I can't pull that off. I'm bad at lying. My tapping feet gives me away,"

"It's true, he's a buster at lying," said Isen.

We all pondered at a solution before Hosse fumbled out a gem of a rose from his pocket and said

"Give this to her. Today's Valentine's Day. It'll cheer her up,"

"Where did you get this?" I asked curious.

"It's called a Humming Rose. The florist said that once you give this to someone, you become linked for life,"

"Well you handed me a Humming Rose. That means we are brothers for life,"

"Well we are not if you wait any longer to give it to Charloette," Hosse pointed his finger out towards her direction.

"Alright I'm going,"

Charloette sat 25 yards across on a swing with her head down staring at her shadow. I tried approaching her with a calm demeanour. But my heart raced into a thunder as I stood before her.

I gathered all courage as I held out the rose before her downturned face. Surprised she looked up with those soul searching green eyes at me.

"What is this?" she inquired.

"A Humming rose. Thought it would cheer you up"

"A rose? You're in your senses right,"

"Yup I surely am. After all who else has the courage to approach you with a rose,"

"Only an idiot like you," she smiled back.

One day is all it took to change our lives. Friends, family and love. Who do you choose when the dice rolls out? Can't imagine me making that sort of decision without flinching. But that's how plucky my buddy Christoff is. Nobody saw a winter was coming. One that wouldn't thaw for a decade. But there were a few moments of meraki and I thank God for that time when the five of us were still together.

"You shouldn't have risked your life?" Charloette spoke earnestly

"It was necessary," Hosse replied hugging her, "Thank God that he was there,"

"All's well that ends well," I pondered for those two.

Meanwhile Isabell and Christoff were into a heated argument.

"You kept me in the dark,"

"We had no time. Besides you wouldn't have agreed,"

"You made me point a gun at you Christoff. Do you know terrified I was? And compound that with Hosse being held captive. Why do you two knuckleheads have to do things in such a reckless way,"

"Calm down Isabell. It all ended well, right," Hosse tried to mediate.

"Well what if it didn't ? You two can't keep giving me these nervous breakdowns. I'm in no condition to tolerate it any more,"

"Well a lawyer argues all the time. These breakdowns are a part of your life," Christoff fooled around.

"Maybe it's normal for a lawyer to argue but not for a mother," Isabell let out the secret at last.

Hearing this Hosse flabbergasted into delight, Christoff zipped up fooling and Charloette cuddled Isabell into an embrace.

"Well how long?" asked a fidgety Hosse

"About a month"

"A month....Goodness gracious I should have known when you avoided that Martini last week,"

"You didn't have a clue either Christoff, did you?" Isabell taunted.

"Yup. Today you indeed outdid me. So as a gift. Hosse is being relieved of his duties from Barrows. He'll work as a manager at Hewlett Designs starting next week,"

"It's not just Hosse. I want you to find a much safer job Christoff. We will need you as her godfather,"

"So it's a girl,"

"Yup I even have a name in mind for her. Sarah."

"That's a lovely name," Hosse admitted.

"It means joyful princess. Kind of suits her," Christoff remarked.

Charloette however remained meekish. Her eyes showed love and our Christoff had not spoken to her since his arrival. Now when their gazes met, I realised they needed time alone.

"Christoff after all this ruckus, I'm gonna need a tumbler to cool down"

I said sighing.

"I was hoping you'd say that buddy. Luckily there's an Inn nearby. Let's go there,"

Just like that Christoff exited the room avoiding Charloette. That lad was still shy. And her green eyes showed yearning. I knew I had to intervene.

"Come Charloette let's leave these soon to be parents alone,"

"Yeah Isen,"

As we walked across the corridor I asked her the inevitable, "Charloette, how long have you known Christoff ?"

"That's a strange question Isen,"

"Answer it,"

"Since childhood,"

"And has he ever been good at speaking out his mind?"

"I guess not,"

"Then what on Earth is stopping you from telling him your feelings? I mean for 2 years you guys didn't meet or talk. And our Christoff is too shy to confess,"

"You're right Isen. Sometimes I feel like smacking that disarming smile off his handsome face. I myself don't even know why I love that buster,"

"If you could reason your way into love, then it isn't love. Funny thing that even our mind tries to justify this utterly nonsensical emotion. But we must not stop loving Charloette. Because love is the best thing we do especially when we have absolutely no clue why?"

"That's deep coming from you Isen,"

"No, these are Mary's words. She asked me to convey it you,"

"Well that's just like her,"

"Mary. She's the string that ties us all no matter where we are," Charloette pondered

"There he is," Isen said as I saw Christoff staring at those streetlights ahead, "I'm leaving you two alone. Tell him. Ok."

"Buddy I've got to bail out. My boss just called in with work," Isen pretended.

"Really. Well this is a first. Isen choosing duty over drinks," Christoff joked.

"Well we all need a first. Don't we?" Isen said looking at me , "Anyway. Goodbye,"

And so here we were. Just the two of us.

Dusk had fallen heavily over the sidewalk as we stood outside the Barrows. There, we waited and waited more for each other to speak. But maybe words weren't the right thing to say.

During my time away I missed him. Every now and then, that jovial face of his evoked a quaint feeling of childhood fondness, but now it had grown beyond that.

Speaking of memories, I remember one particular day very vividly.

I was in college when I had the chance to visit Riviera on a fortnight holiday. That was the time of our first reunion which I distinctly remember for one reason. On my arrival at the Little Angels, everyone greeted me with warmth. Still there was this one insensitive jackass of Christoff Myers who was missing.

"Searching for someone?" asked Isen.

"You know who," I said in nostalgia

"Same old Christoff. He's never on time,"

"Well, he'll meet us at the station," said Hosse.

"Station?"

"We're going to Seren on an excursion. You may want to join along,"

"Sure,"

That night the atmosphere on the dinner table felt uplifting. Talks of all the time spent apart, to the future that everyone worked for, it was a very optimistic tone. But it wasn't always like this. There were days when on the dinner table we had a few breadcrumbs, grapes and a glass of milk. Children we were, during those gloomy days when Mary and the others were struggling to look after us.

As everyone sat eating absent minded with their own thoughts, there was a certain kid who would put two grapes midway between his throat and carry out a mighty impressive act of apparent choking.

Mary would then immediately rush to his side and all the children would encircle that idiot.

"Hiccup Hi….cup,"

"How many times I'll tell you not to swallow grapes without chewing," said an anxious Mary.

And just when he's about to get treated, he would shoot out two grapes straight at Isen's belly, gobble up the rebounds before chewing them and gulping down instantly.

"Just like this Grandma," he would say in an innocent voice.

Those theatrics made us laugh and what better remedy to tough times than laughing it off.

"Yeah just like that," said a cheered up Mary.

"He's still a kid. But he's grown so mature," said Martha to Mary.

"He learns fast. To let out all the sadness with a hiccup and let in all the smiles with a rebound. I never thought he'd teach me my own lessons," said Mary looking at that hopeful kid.

And now I sit looking at an empty chair, reserved should Christoff drop in.

"He'll be there. Scold him as much as you want," said Mary realizing my gaze.

The next morning we found ourselves on the train bound to Seren. Two minutes to leave the platform and he still hadn't arrived.

"What is that idiot doing?"

"He's a trainee at the Barrows car repair facility. He has just joined in along with Jeffrey," said Isen.

"Still…" I was interrupted by the whistle of the train.

"We're leaving," Hosse joined us at the train's entrance.

With a tortoise pace the wheels had started rolling as I gave a sigh of despair.

"Dimwit," I scolded him.

As soon as I gave up hope and turned towards the bogie than a loud beeping sound sizzled into my ear.

In a red classic jumper there stood Christoff and Jeffrey in the backseat with a chauffeur driving at the wheels trying to match the train's slowly picking speed.

"Those two morons do know how to make an entrance," remarked Hosse.

In a frantic manner that car kept beeping as it drove alongside the train's platform causing upheaval.

"You crazy madmen," shouted one pedestrian as he narrowly dodged the racing car.

"Sorry," shouted Jeffrey.

"John Trueman on my count of three you'll slow down and sync," instructed Christoff.

They stood on the backseat and went beyond us.

"Can't we just stop the train?"

"Nope. No hand stops on this Seren Express" countered Isen.

"Ok 1,2 and three. Punch it," shouted Christoff as they synced with the train's speed.

"Christoff, make it quick, we are running out of platform" said a petrified Jeffrey looking forwards.

"Isen, move back,"

It was the nervous Jeffrey who first made the jump into the Seren's entrance.

"John, thank you," said Christoff before stepping into the train in a much composed manner.

"Whew…. that was close," said Jeffrey still trembling.

"Just on time," Christoff shrugged off the incident in his suave manner.

At this I gave a slight punch on Christoff's head saying, "Stop smiling, you car jumping monkey,"

"That hurt," complained a childlike Christoff.

His theatrics had gotten better with passing time. So much so that Isen and I kept laughing about it all the way through.

"Still a buster," I said to him.

"I'm sorry to keep you waiting,"

"Your actions made up for it Christoff. Just don't do it ever again,"

"Sure,"

The fellowship of our journey was now complete. Christoff Myers, Isen Hughes, Charloette Whitman, Jeffrey Spiegel and Hosse Jean Hoffman. We were close friends. And this excursion couldn't get any better.

"So who was that driver?"

"That is John. He's a trainee like us,"

"That red jumper. Whose idea was it?"

"No one's. We were stuck in the traffic so we just drove into the platform before we saw the train leaving,"

"Improvisation huh. That's cool"

Amongst all the cheer and mirth, I felt the journey was too short. Yes many things were discussed, and yet there was a mystique about Christoff that intrigued me. His eyes they had changed. They knew how to lie in front of Mary. But not before me.

"The Barrows, you say. What do you learn there?"

"Basics of taking down a dilapidated car, fixing it, and selling it as a brand new cherry,"

"Is that so? Say that looking into my eyes again,"

"Why would I do that?"

"Because your left leg is tapping the floor. Your eyes aren't blinking. And most of all you didn't stop. It's pre-emptive,"

"Nope. It's the truth," he played smart. But that was it.

I was having none of this anymore.

"I didn't say it was a lie. If you need to keep it close to your vest, keep it. But never pretend before me,"

"Ok…you soul searching detective. I'll tell you about it in due time,"

However it was the last that we ever talked about his profession.

Reminiscing, we now strolled along the sidewalk, talking over trivial things, deliberately avoiding the crux of our hearts, before my gaze fixated onto a sparkling bouquet of flowers.

Without any word I broke off from the conversation and headed straight to the florist.

"Where you're going?" said Christoff turning backwards after he noticed my absence.

"The roses. I want to buy one."

There I bought just one rose. But it was beautiful. The man called it the Humming Rose for some reason that I didn't bother to ask.

"Shining and cool," remarked Christoff.

"Just like me," I said before putting the blue glistening rose inside my lapel.

"Give me one as well," said Christoff as he bought a rose.

"So what do we do now?" I asked him after we walked aimlessly into the night.

"Let's make a wish. You do remember the Fountain of Gilmore. Well they've shifted it but I guess it still grants wishes," he said with nostalgia.

The fountain now lay beside the Riviera Lake. Back in the old days, we would drop a coin wishing it to bring us good luck.

The lake seemed serene enshrouded by the overhanging pine trees. Amidst the centre of an impromptu replica of the Stonehenge, stood

Gilmore. There was a flight of steps that spiralled to the top of the statue pretty high up near to the branches of a pine tree that was decorated with neon coins overhanging from their tips.

"I wonder if the architect designed it to prevent old people from wishing here," I joked.

"Sophistication catches the eye but only if simplicity isn't compromised,"

"That's deep. But yeah it would be better if we could just drop a coin standing from the ground,"

But as we reached the top of the platform there we found a message carved against the bark.

"To the old and the young, do watch the sky up north as you drop the coin,"

"Ok let's try this. I'm curious to see what the architect has designed," I said before plucking a neon coin.

"Me too,"

As we closed our eyes to wish, the coin started to feel heavy. With passing time it felt as if our wishes were weighing it down. Then as we opened our eyes and dropped those coins, a bright flash emanated behind us. A splash of water echoed in as we saw a glistening star falling across the expanse of the clear night sky before landing into the Riviera Lake.

I inched nearer to the pine tree to catch a better glimpse of the star. But sadly it had vanished.

"Any explanation Christoff?"

"Sure. Just some echoing amplifiers created by encircling pine trees connected to a microphone near to the fountain surface. Couple that to a hidden hologram projection, it feels real as if a star really fell down to grant your wish,"

"Nice deduction. So what did you wish for?"

"You don't disclose your wish, Charloette. It's personal all the way through,"

"Well I wished for a union," I said aloud.

"Perhaps it may get granted seeing you don't mind voicing your wish," said Christoff as a call interrupted our conversation and it so happened that my wish might have already been granted.

It was 10'0 clock when Charloette and I arrived at Caverly Inn.

"Jeff's treating then?" she asked.

"Yup. It's his b'day. All are waiting. Let's go in,"

As we entered in we found our friends seated at the corner table. There was Cara, Evans, Hugo, Alice, Noira, Stephen, and our buddy Jeff. Two seats had been reserved for us.

The fellowship was now complete and we had a sumptuous dinner coupled with pep talks and hopes for the future. But the reason for which I remember that day is different.

It was the day of the Piper's Kiss.

As I tried my best to lighten up the occasion something unexpected happened.

The florist guy from evening was sitting on a table opposite to us and looking at a lady behind the counter nervously.

"He likes her," I said unconsciously.

"What?" said Jeffrey.

"Nothing,"

I saw he was holding a sort of a small present in his clenched hand.

"Excuse me for a minute," I told them and walked to the florist's table.

Taking a seat in front of him, I said, "It's a ring, isn't it?"

At first he didn't remember me but eventually a bulb lit in his head.

"You!" he exclaimed in surprise.

"Shh. Don't speak loudly. Now how long have you known that lady?"

"What lady?" he played innocent

"Look I'm no love expert. But the way you look at her, it's clear you like her,"

"But I don't know if she does,"

"Listen, it's better to have confessed your feelings and being let down, than to never get the opportunity to do so,"

"You know. I'm elder to you, but you seem wiser," he said with a smile.

"Nah age doesn't give wisdom. Experience does,"

"I think I'll go and propose to her,"

"No no wait. Does she know you?"

"Yes, she's my neighbour. She's currently studying to be a doctor and does part time here to pay for her study,"

"Well, that's interesting, but let's withhold the ring. How about a flower?"

"A flower. I don't have one,"

"What a stupid florist you are!.... Know what, I have the perfect flower,"

I searched my frock coat pocket and finally took out a rose.

"The Humming Roses," he said in delight.

"Okay you told me I'll find it to be of some use. Go and give this to her,"

He did as I told him and this is what happened.

The lady at the counter was very pretty. So at first the florist stumbled for words but he spoke

"Trisha,"

The lady looked at him and instantly there was a gleam in her eyes.

"Nicholas," she said in a merry voice, "what are you doing here?"

"I....I just...came to give you this,"

He showed her the rose and an expression of love was evident.

"It's beautiful," she said taking the rose from his hand.

Usually such moments call for drinks and my role was perfect for this. I walked to the shop owner's side and chatted with him.

"You know. How about free drinks to all, from that man?" I asked him handing in the money.

"Anything special to be done," said he.

"Certainly. The lady over your counter. Give her this wine, but make sure this ring is in it,"

"Anything else,"

"Yes,"

The arrangements were done and one would wonder why so much fuss over giving a ring. But here's the thing. You can't simply waltz in and give your neighbour a ring and propose her. The atmosphere needs to be created. Remember no matter how much a woman loves a man, she always wants him to not only make the first advance but also to do so in grandeur and elegance.

And my florist guy here was too simple for this sort of a thing. Thus I chose to help him a bit.

I took my seat beside Jeffrey and they inquired about my little adventure.

"I know you have a lot of questions, but wait," I told them.

Within five minutes glasses full of wine were placed at each table and the counter.

"What's this?" Trisha asked the waiter.

"It's from this man," he said looking at Nicholas.

Obviously Nicholas was as much surprised as her, but he kept nerve.

"It's from you?" she asked him.

"Ye..Yes. Today's your birthday,"

"Thank you,"

She slowly drank the wine and I feared that she might gulp the ring down. But luckily it didn't happen. Only when a sip remained she noticed it and a surprise came over her face,"

"Nic..." she said startled.

That's when all the lights in the shop went out and the limelight fell straight onto Trisha and Nicholas.

The waiter gave me the mic and I announced the proposal.

"Everybody. Mr. Nicholas here wants to propose to Miss Trisha. So I request all of you to support this lad with your best wishes,"

The musician played out the Valentine's special and everybody cheered in unison, "Trisha, please accept Nicholas's ring,"

I noticed Trisha's face going red and a lovely smile adorned her already beautiful face just like a star to complete the masterpiece of a decorated Christmas tree.

Slowly but surely Nicholas got caught in the act and asked her," Will you marry me, Trisha?"

The music died down. Silence ensued the following moments and all our breaths were drawn in until she spoke

"Yes,"

Suddenly the lights went back on. The music started playing once again and a roar of applause resounded the Inn.

My job here was done. As we were leaving, Nicholas and Trisha shared a kiss.

"You are indeed a difficult guy to understand," said Charloette as we friends bade goodbye.

"Why is that?" I asked intrigued

At this she gave a sigh and held my hands, "Let's walk to the Little Angels,"

As our fingers intertwined an inexplicable warmth resounded in me. I had seen her smile a million times before but tonight her soulful eyes were sparkling with joy and conviction.

We walked and we walked with hesitation in our minds. So much that no words were spoken. Yet a bond was forged that night, one that would stand the test of time.

"So this is it," Charloette said as we stood before the orphanage.

"Yep. Greet Mary for me," I said before turning to leave.

Just then a tug of her hands pulled me towards her as I felt her breath whisking past my face. And before I could speak she kissed me into brightening.

That moment is the best memory that only I remember. I relive it every day. It's this hope that gives meaning to my life.

As she withdrew an honest smile blossomed on her face.

"Always wanted to do that," she finally confessed.

"Charloette…"

"Christoff Myers. I love you. Always have and always will. Thank you for being in my life,"

With this she ran off into the house not waiting to hear my reply.

Thus the story of the Piper's kiss concluded. That day I realized that love is wonderful. It's painful, it's fanciful and is the only opium one needs to live life by. Surely it has sacrifices but know this love is its own reward.

Polaris

It was a day before the engagement, at 7 in the evening, did I receive a call. I picked it up and guess who greeted me.

"Christoff, its Hosse.... I was wondering if you could come to the Hugo Gowns. You see, I'm having some trouble selecting Isabell's dress,"

"...Ok then. I'll meet you there in an hour,"

"Thank you," he replied and ended the call.

It was in the twilight hour when I met Hosse. The two gowns that vendor showed us were equally brilliant. But none were as attractive and beautiful as this one gown that I had seen earlier.

It stood on the mannequin facing the window and whoever had designed it, must have certainly possessed some outclassed brilliance.

"This one looks good," I said to vendor.

"That one sir. It's a classic but ladies nowadays prefer these modern ones," said the man

"Well, modern or classic, that gown is certainly perfect. I think we'll buy that," said Hosse

Thus, it was decided and the gown bought.

"Well thank you for coming here," he said as we stood outside by the door.

"It's okay," I said and took leave.

I kept strolling aimlessly on the pavement, maybe for ten or fifteen minutes when Hosse's voice hailed me from the back.

I turned round and saw him breathing heavily.

"What happened?" I asked curious.

"...I just received a call from the decor manager....He needs my help to setup something. So can you give this to Isabell, please?"

"..Sure," I said after pondering for a while. He told me her address and then left again in hurry.

While I walked towards her home, many thoughts invaded my mind, and there without even knowing I stood before her gate. Coming to a halt, I composed myself.

"I'll leave as soon as I give this to her," I told myself.

Ascending those little flight of seven steps, was arduous. And now I stood on the front porch, ringing at the bell.

When the door opened I was greeted by Isabell who looked ecstatic.

"Hosse called a while ago. He said you'd come," she spoke in her lively manner, "Come inside,"

"Nope. I must leave," I insisted.

"Christopher you have never visited us. Please, stay here for a while," she requested.

"I can't. I have some..." But before I could speak she interrupted me and in her honest pleading voice said

"For me, please,"

Her eyes were staring expectantly, and I could see that she wished for me to stay.

"Okay," I complied.

"Thank you," she said in merriment and holding me by the hand led me in.

Her home was luxurious and pristine. But above all her parents were really noble and loving.

"Hello there, young man. It's nice to have finally met you," said her father.

"Yes, Isabell often talks about you," complimented her mother.

"Well, it's really nice of you to say that. But in reality, she's a good person for which she holds me in such regard," I replied.

"I told you he was full of wisdom," said Isabell as she took a seat beside me.

"Yes, he is," said her mother.

"So Christoff, I know it's a personal question but when do you propose on getting married?"

"Well sir, I haven't found the girl yet. When I do, and if fate allows then I certainly will,"

"Still single," joked Isabell.

"It's a permanently temporary thing," I replied.

"But still. Give us some idea of what sort of girl you like. Who knows we might know such a girl?"

"It's embarrassing you know,"

"No, it isn't. Tell us," urged her mother.

"...Someone who would trust me no matter what I did...Yet have the guts to slap me hard on the face when I err...Yes someone whose love for me is as evident from her care as it is from her anger,"

"Well that's really difficult to find," Isabell replied.

And so, the night passed by where her family gave me the privilege to have dinner with them, and there afterwards I had the will to mend my way back home with my tired soul.

As I lay on my bed, I reflected when I said that I had not found her.

"I lied. Charloette and I had not talked since I left the orphanage for the Barrows. But her face always loomed before my eyes. She is too precious and I can't lose her. I knew I won't always be there to protect her,"

Soon the day of engagement came. We had finished our work early and were now at our apartment.

"The gift, where is it?" I asked.

"It's with Grandma. When we dropped her that day, we forgot the gift that was in her bag," said Jeffrey.

"Ok. Then we better get ready fast,"

"Yup,"

Dressed in our neatest attires, we left home and hired a cab. It took 2 hours to reach Mary's place. She was waiting for us outside with the gift.

The cab stopped right in front of her, and I opened the glass pane to see Mary dressed in her usual attire, "Grandma, what's wrong? Aren't you coming?"

"No, I can't come. A child's sick," she told me.

"The caretakers can look after the child," I said.

"Nope. There's only Margaret with me. All the others are out on various errands,"

"Isabell will feel bad,"

"Nope she'll understand. Give her this gift, and tell her my blessings are with her,"

She handed me the gift and we left hurriedly in our cab.

It took us a long time to reach Avenue Island. But it was worth the journey. The place was decorated like a queen's palace. A huge lavish banquet was laid in the middle of a lawn whose laurel bushes were spangled with glowing lights. Now all this we saw as we were descending down a hill track. Avenue Island was actually a lagoon.

The gate that welcomed the visitors stood illuminating the darkness around and when you entered in, you'd find yourself not on a well paved road but on a pier above a water track. Both the sides were covered in a canopy of trees and extended quite some distance. A Gondola was kept ready to take us to the party.

As we sailed the canopy cover slowly vanished out of our sight and there a villa that exuded grandeur and majesty stood in the middle of a gigantic green light-illuminated lawn.

We alighted down and searched for our friends. Luckily, we found Hosse who greeted us in warm delight.

"Glad, you two came so early," he said sarcastically.

"Yes. We are gladder, believe us," said Jeffrey.

"Where's Isabell?" I asked.

"Yes. She's there on the lawn surrounded by guests,"

Hosse meanwhile left us to attend to another guest. We walked towards the mob of people that encircled our friend. As we pushed our way forward, I caught a glimpse of her.

The gown that I had seen on that day suited her wonderfully. She looked like an angel. The fairest maiden in the country.

As she saw us, she excused herself from everyone else's company and approached us.

"You two. I have been waiting for you so long," she said.

"Yes. Here, Grandma gave this," I said handing her the gift.

Before she could reply, a guest interrupted us and we were blotted out of her sight, by her relatives.

"Seems like she's happy," said Jeffrey.

"Yes, she indeed is," I replied.

We walked about admiring the place and finally joined in others at the banquet.

"Yum. The food's delicious," said Jeffrey as we stood near a corner in the dimly lit space.

"Yeah eat all you can,"

We stood there and ate heartily. But I must confess that my friend is a deep eater and in no time his plate had been emptied after which he went off to fetch more food

So I stood there alone, with my back against the dark sky, analysing everybody. That's when a voice caught me by surprise.

"You finally came," a feminine voice said.

I turned to my side and found her dressed in a red gown. She appeared strikingly attractive. Fair complexion coupled with a brunette's hair and a shimmering face that complemented her killer green eyes.

"Hi…" That was all I could say.

"2 years. No contact. And the only thing you say on seeing me is hi," Charloette seemed piqued.

I didn't have an answer to that. So, like all wise school children do on being questioned I chose to remain silent.

"Christoff, snap out of your doldrums," said Charloette waving her hands.

"Yeah," I seemed to have come back to reality at last.

"You stargazing buffoon, let's take a walk," she said as she took me by my arms and led me to the sidewalk that encircled Avenue Falls.

"So, how's work?"

"Uh…Well we repair cars all day round. It's pretty boring actually,"

"You always wanted to travel. So how come you've decided to settle?"

"Well things change you know,"

"Nah. With you nothing changes," she said with a smile.

"What does that mean?"

"It means you still can't lie," she said stopping before me.

"You saw my tapping feet, huh,"

"Yep. Which is why I want to know this?" she finally held onto my weak nerve.

"Do you love me Christoff?"

I swear that for one moment time stood still. The noises faded into oblivion and all I could feel was the intensity of her gaze searching my soul for her answer.

The rhythm that makes my heart beat stood right in front me questioning my hesitation every time the thought of an amatory relationship arose. I couldn't lie. Neither could I tell the truth. Silence was the only answer I could give. But gosh, I could never stop Charloette from reading my mind.

"Sometimes words aren't the right thing to say. Right Christoff," she said with an enigmatic smile.

"Thank you," I replied.

"You should thank Mary for that. Christoff, I know you've got your secrets but don't live your entire life alone. You preach about love and hope to everyone but you've built a fortress of solitude to guard yourself from sharing it with anyone,"

"It is my life's paradox Charloette,"

"Then I do hope that someday that paradox gets broken," she whispered gently.

"Maybe one day it will. Now enough about me, what's going on in your life?"

"I'm still wandering. There's a part of me that wants to see how vast this world is, and then there's a part that seeks a place that it can call home,"

"Why not do it both?"

"Wouldn't that be greedy?"

"Not at all. The heart seeks what it seeks. You're a free soul with an unmatched zest for life,"

"Says the reserved guy with an unparalleled view of this world," she replied in grace.

"You still remember, huh,"

"Seeming opposites destined to part. How can I forget those words Christoff? That fortune teller's prophecy has been etched into my memory and I can't find a way to let go of it,"

This piqued me a bit. Coming to an abrupt halt, I held Charloette by her hand. Pulling her towards me I took her by surprise. Those green eyes showed tears of conflict as our breaths intermingled in that cold breeze. Caressing her hair back onto her ear, I reminded her of our resolve which had made the fortune teller declare in delight

"Her phoenix winged hope and that titanium clad resolve of yours will indeed change not only yours but the destiny of this world,"

"You refuse to give up on me, don't you?" declared a mellowed girl whose pluckiness life had stolen.

"Even when those wings get chained Charloette, burn them if you must and set yourself free. Phoenix rise from their ashes, and so must your zest for life,"

Those welled up tears finally watered down her red cheeks as she embraced me crying.

"Don't you ever leave me again,"

"I'm sorry,"

"You left without a word. Didn't answer my calls, refused to meet me, kept dodging any approach I made to contact you. Maybe all of this wouldn't have hurt so much if it weren't for the time, we spent together that spring,"

"We all have our reasons, Charloette. Once the time is right, I'll tell you everything,"

"I hate you Myers," she said affectionately.

"Who else can a lovely girl like you can hate, except me?"

"Stupid, you don't understand a thing about my hatred,"

The wind had been rising as cheers started inundating the chilly air that felt ever so warm by her embrace. That was the last time I held her in my arms, before fate took her away from me. Or rather I distanced my beat away from her heart.

Jeff has this eerie tendency of barging in at the wrong moment. But I thank God he did that day on Avenue Islands. Christoff Myers had been reminded of his true name. And that didn't bode well. Every time Charloette calls him by his christened name, he has to hold himself back from revealing the truth of her identity to her. She was not an orphan. And Hosse knew it all.

"Jeff, you geeky moron, you came at the right time. Maybe your destiny's about to change."

"Uh huh…," he smiled at Charloette who remained meekish after she had withdrawn.

"Hitler has fallen in love with a Jew. That too a pearl of a dame. The Irish wolves are howling. For the moon shines bluest tonight. Never thought hatred could hide an unfathomable love," Jeff said gazing at Charloette.

"Mate, one of these days I'll set those wolves onto you," I jousted back.

"...Hope you do. 'Coz you're a live bait buddy. You know what I mean," Jeff said looking at the congregation ahead.

"Gosh I love such weddings. Let's join them. And Charloette. Be yourself. That spunky tomboy spirit veiled underneath your elysian charm will see you through with what's about to unfold tonight,"

"What do you mean?" she asked with sparking curiosity.

"Nah. You'll decipher that. I know it, you will," I said leaving her bepuzzled.

"Christoff..." Jeff spoke gravely.

"Ease down buddy. No one will get hurt,"

"Idiot I know that. It's you he's after," he paused midway.

"Exactly....so let's get the ball rolling,"

"Think about this bait thing. We can use a decoy,"

"No. The first time, we got saved. He targeted her. Can't risk it again,"

"An open invitation to a sniper. A live bomb, a fire, all hell is about to break lose,"

"We'll first attend the wedding. So, you better put on a smile, pal,"

Hosse and Isabell stood at the altar completely immersed in their wedding vows. Before them stood this gathering of distinguished folks. The futuristic entrepreneurs, flamboyant technicians of Polaris, inventors of Wright Pyrotechnics, statesmen from all walks of society, and not to forget the heir to Brethren Court of this country. And our job was to ensure the smooth conduct of this ceremony.

"Do you Hosse Jean Hoffman take Isabell Foster as your lawfully wedded wife?" said the priest awaiting my brother's reply, who stood their dumbstruck.

He was frightfully pensive. After all we had chosen his wedding day to set a trap for the man behind the Greenwich Bombings.

"Yo, Hosse get this thing rolling. Even a turtle will crawl back faster into the sea," I chipped in onto his concealed microphone.

"...Yes, I do," he said softly.

"Gosh look at him. The most outspoken guy amongst us troublemakers, has forgotten how to talk," Jeff joined in as well to lighten up this rare occasion.

"Forget talking, he's getting a lifetime's worth of criticism after this gets over. Poor chap. Not even a moment into wedlock, and his blabbering flirtatious mouth gets zip-locked," joked Stephen as he surveyed the area from the chapel's attic window.

"Hosse. That's a married guy's perspective. Any cheeky one liner, you'd like to add," I kept peppering him.

Sadly, he couldn't reply. He was amidst his wedding vow and we were pulling his legs. That was one memory, we'd reminisce down the line.

Meanwhile the priest asked Isabell, "Do you take this man as your lawfully wedded husband?"

Silence ensued for a moment as everyone including Hosse stared at Isabell with their breaths drawn in anticipation of her reply.

"Yes I do," she replied after a deliberate pause which I had requested from her.

This evoked a comic sigh of relief from Hosse, which made me withhold my laughter.

"Christoff, you did that," Evans deduced. He was in charge of those miniscule explosions.

"Yes. Now let's get serious. 27 minutes guys. Evans, you'll set the extradition rolling with those diversions. Jeff meanwhile will secure all exits from Avenue Islands. Stephen will snipe out the target as soon as I lure him out. The logistic team waiting at the docks, they'll help with the evacuation. And Hosse, yours is the simplest job. Get ready to take a bullet for your beloved wife,"

The ceremony went as planned. Our pals were married. People were now dining at the banquet as Hosse kept near Isabell. It was almost time.

"60 seconds. I'll present the gift. Stephen and Evans be ready,"

I advanced to the centre of the lawn where the couple stood. Stephen kept close watch for any unforeseen movement. There was none.

"The gift. Take it out of your pocket Christoff,"

I looked around for the girl who was the key to our plan. Charloette stood at the vicinity of a Yew tree conversing. I gazed at her as she grasped my presence. Her eyebrows flashed as her gentle smile got reciprocated by mine.

"Let's begin,"

No sooner did I take out the gift, a man dressed in suit charged forward.

"9 o clock," alerted Stephen.

Evans instinctively activated the first charge. An explosion at the podium created ample mayhem.

The assaulter's focus shifted for a moment. And as he turned, Stephen fired a shot meticulously through that crowd straight to the side of his neck.

"One down, four more to go. Feral blow from your 7. Take guard," the sniper instructed.

I swooped down evading the punch before knocking his knees out. The rest was Steph's work as he took him out midway through his fall.

Meanwhile Hosse kept guard near Isabell as a second detonation directed the confused crowd down to the bay side of Avenue Island.

"Jeff, secure the exit,"

"Already in position,"

"Good,"

Now came the tricky part. The switch. Its objective to relay the device to Isabell.

Hosse had quickly slipped in the package as the three of us headed towards the north side of the cathedral ground where Charloette was.

"What's with the explosions and those men who assaulted you?" asked a tense girl.

"No idea. Trying to stay alive," I said outright, "Now do you have a handkerchief in your purse?"

"No. I don't carry a purse," she replied confused, "You already know that,"

"Here take this," said Isabell as she took one from her husband's lapel.

I gave Hosse a knowing glance as the two women tried to grasp the situation, we had led them into.

"Hosse. The one incoming on your left?" said Steph.

"Affirmed. He's the brother,"

"He has a gun in his back pocket. Take cover,"

"Isabell and Charloette move quickly behind that tree. Now," I shouted as I donned those dreaded gloves, "Hosse on the count of three, duck,"

Alejandro was his name aka Aleksi. He ran a cartel on behalf of his brother Diego de la Vega better known by his codename Diego. He went rogue 4 years back. And it was his position the Barrows had recruited me into.

"One, he grabs hold of a magnum. Two, he takes aim. Three, the gun cocks as he puts his finger on the trigger,"

A wailing gunshot enshrouds the vicinity as Hosse ducks just in time. He takes another aim but this time he finds a wire round his wrist. I activate the charge as a high voltage current singed his arms making him drop his gun.

"Dart him out," I mic out to Steph.

"Hosse, the vest's on, right,"

"I'm steaming hot. Take me out," said he regaining his jesting demeanour.

"Save that for later,"

Evans had lit the penultimate charge in the cathedral. It's objective to divert our friends to the citadel.

"I've taken out the fourth one. The last one's yours," said Steph as he kept aim on Hosse's brooch underneath which lay a pack of blood.

Yuvisko Helinsky was our target. Orchestrator of that merciless genocide. His presence here was guaranteed by the device I relayed to

Hosse. Its passcode lay in Charloette's mind. One I had intentionally reinforced throughout our years together.

Pandemonium rocked this wedding night as the cathedral came crumbling down. Our trio kept advancing towards the citadel where the final act was planned.

"10 o' clock. Black dressed man with auburn locks. He's your guy," Jeff relayed in.

"The rescue boats are ready, Jeff. Get the brethren guy out. I'll intercept our target at the entrance,"

There was a bunker underneath the citadel manor. Adjacent to that lay a tunnel which led to the lakeside where our rescue boat was waiting on stand-by.

"Hosse lead them into the northern corridor. There is an iron doorway at the end of a right-hand passage. Get them into that before the collapse," I relayed on intercom.

Yuvisko was rushing towards the stony entrance that overhung the iconic Manor that had witnessed the wedding of Monarchs. It stood the weathering of centuries and countless wars on which this country stood. A beacon of craftsmanship to the architect of yesteryears.

"What a pity to blow this heritage to smithereens!" said Evans.

"We do what is required. Keep your feelings aside," I replied.

As the auburn-haired guy advanced, I charged up the gloves before encircling the wire onto his neck. Instantly his hands froze on the hinge, as he understood what he had gotten himself into.

"It's a pleasure to have finally met you," he said unfazed before turning towards me.

Crimson coloured eyes ominously stared at me as a cold breeze swirled up this "Night of Frenzy" towards an unexpected conclusion.

"Where is Diego?" I inquired.

"The device, you have, has it all," he replied unflinchingly.

"Why is he after it?"

"The entire world is after it. One way or another you will have to choose Christopher,"

"I have already chosen,"

"That is good. For your mettle will be tested to its core,"

Indeed, he was right. The aftermath made it to media's front-page. My decision made a grand mess of a plan that had been executed meticulously up to that point.

"Christoff, the passage is secure," informed Jeff.

"Rig it out," I said before cutting off all communications.

I let go of the nape and retracted the wire. A choice made in the moment that sealed the fate of countless individuals.

"Turn yourself in,"

"Why?"

"Because you're innocent,"

Imminent explosions shook the Island as the monument came crumbling down. Meanwhile, Hosse led the girls out of the tunnel where we were supposed to rendezvous. Steph would keep a hawk's eye on his brooch as they exit onto the little creek before making their way to the shoreline. Jeff must have ensured the return of all guests to mainland. All that remained was for Evans to ferry the rescue boat.

Diego is a vagabond. His association with the Barrows was brief. But during his tenure he earned himself the moniker of Panther. All his extraditions were immaculate. In reality he was the spearhead of a project called Polaris. His objective to ensure the safety of one man. Its creator. Yet, for unverified reasons that two decades project was scraped. Sources say it was due to the death of Newman Reeds, the man Diego was supposed to protect. Some say it was he who killed him. The matter is rife with speculations since all research work went missing. Its resurgence was due to the discovery of a data drive that was mailed anonymously to our intelligence wing. It was encoded. Any means to retrieve it would render it a useless stick. Only one attempt was possible. And at the centre of it all lay the name of one girl to whom it was addressed to. Charloette Whitman.

"You relayed the access key to me," I spoke succinctly.

"And you destroyed it," said Yuvisko.

"It's criminal to have such power,"

"Governments have toppled in its search. Newman unknowingly tapped into it. That led to his demise,"

"He encoded it using her genome,"

"Rightly gauged. Still, you unwittingly imprinted the access key into her memory,"

"One's memories cannot be retrieved. It's the safest of all safes in the world,"

"No matter what, Diego will come after her,"

"We'll see. Right now, you are framed for the Greenwich incident. Turn yourself in. We'll ensure your amnesty,"

"Assuring words. You seem calm given the vexing circumstances,"

"It's a tradition amongst us. We always keep our end of the deal no matter what it takes,"

"Alright, let's do what we were here for,"

"I lost contact with Myers," shouted Evans as it drizzled down

Waves grew restless as this night progressed. There was no sign of Christoff as they advanced along that beaten track. Jutting landscape silhouetted their way as a dim light from the ferry awaited them.

"We go ahead with the plan," Steph said on mic, "I'm taking aim,"

"Wait until she puts on that trench coat," said Evans before handing them out their clothing. As soon as Charloette stepped onto the ferry, Steph sizzled down a bullet straight onto Hosse's brooch. A deafening gunshot startled the seabirds into frenzy as blood gushed out spilling all over Isabell.

The impact nonetheless would take Hosse out. It was within that split second, he was supposed to slip that device into her top pocket. And boy he did it convincingly.

Charloette lay stunned as she witnessed the pool of blood her brother was mired in. She attempted alighting down but Evans promptly intervened.

"Stay here and take cover against the mast," he said holding her back.

Rushing out he led a dazed Isabell into the boat before attending to Hosse who lay unconscious atop the rocks.

"He's heavy," complained Evans

"Nah. You're skinny," said Steph," Quickly haul that newly wedded bum out of here,"

"No sign of Christoff,"

"Not in half a mile," Steph surveyed using the sniping telescope, "That guy likes screwing a perfectly enacted extradition,"

"Maybe he's improvising,"

"God knows what he's got on his mind. Just get them back to Riviera. We'll sort this out on mainland,"

As the ferry waded out into the waters, Steph took a lighter from his back pocket before lighting a cigarette.

"Gosh, it's a cold night. Avenue Islands decimated in order to relay Polaris," Stephen pondered taking in a snuff.

Vows

"Night of Frenzy," Isabell reminisced as we sat on the dinner table, "That's our wedding day's highlight,"

"The media blows it out of proportion," Hosse remarked.

"Half of Avenue Island was blown away. A national heritage. It was that big a scandal,"

"Everything worked out fine. The bomber guy was caught. Hosse made it back alive. No one was harmed," I said before digging in into the pasta.

"Easy for you to say. You are always missing on crucial occasions. Where were you that night?" she asked.

"With Jeff as he helped with the evacuation,"

"What about those two years when you literally went ghost?" asked Isabell.

"Work needed me to travel anonymously,"

At this she gave a wry smile before replying

"You and your secrets,"

"Well. It's a scrumptious dinner you have prepared," I said diverting.

"You are complimenting the wrong person," Isabell glanced towards Charloette.

"Really. You did all of this. I'm surprised,"

"As if you've never eaten anything I've cooked before," she taunted back.

"Yeah. The food is delightfully tasty. Please cheer up a bit,"

She remained listless.

I gestured onto to my pals who gave a clear indication. Charloette had professed her feelings and was waiting for mine. Realizing this the two of them quietly left us alone at the dinner table. I cleared my throat, summoned all my spirit and let it all out.

"Someone who lands you in outrageous problems yet helps you to overcome the cocoon you are trapped in. The one who makes you feel this contradiction of

I lovingly hate you

Who makes you question yourself-

Why am I still tagging along with this imbecile?

Who makes you say this-

I can travel all over the world but can find not a single person like you.

That someone is your destined comrade. A comrade whose company you'd want to cherish for eternity"

I held her hands and finally looked at those soulful eyes

"Charloette, you are my destined comrade. I love you more than you'll ever know. But just this once I need you to know that my life is you,"

The confession came after 21 years of platonic relationship. It welled her up with tears as we sat there with our brows cradled against each other smiling.

"Charl, come with me,"

I held her hands and walked into the living room.

"Hosse and Isabell, we need to tell you something,"

Both of them had noticed the change which was evident in their expression.

Hosse was holding back on his exuberance while Isabell's eyes were gleaming with joy.

It was a much-awaited moment. Both of them had cajoled us throughout our childhood, and now here we were.

"We love each other and would like to be together,"

Hosse gestured towards Isabell as both of them approached us quietly.

Standing at an arm's length in multitudes of silence, they sort of surveyed us. A classic move of theirs to test out one's resolve.

We stood our ground hand in hand.

A minute later all their solemnness turned into festivity.

"Thank God, this day finally arrived," said Isabell, "You two surely kept us waiting,"

"Seeing you two together like this, gives us immense joy. Everyone knows about you. Yet like Mary says some choices have to be made by the children themselves,"

"Sure enough she's wise and kind," said Charloette.

"You two really need to come up with a new trick. This FBI interrogation stare is old school," I cheeked in.

"Maybe it is. But it works all the time. Admit it both of you were nervous," said Isabell.

"We were for a moment. I could hear our breaths and feel my beat. That's when he clasped my hands tighter. It felt assuring," Charloette replied.

"Remember this. With a trusted companion by your side, nothing is as scary as it appears to be. Life's a walk with many twists and turns, hold on to that hand and never let go,"

"Yes, vow to never let go no matter what," said Hosse.

"We do," said our united voice.

It was nearing dusk as first snow of this season started falling. Our afternoon was spent at the theatre where 'A Nightingale' was being screened. This was our first movie together. Probably the most uninterrupted time we had ever spent. With her so close, I felt her emotions as she experienced the nuances of this period drama. Her laughter, her silence as she watched engrossed, her sobbing as she held onto her tears made for a fun day. By the time it finished her head lay atop my shoulder. It was a warm tender feeling.

"How was the movie?" she asked.

"Soulful,"

"I loved it to my core. Down the years, this will become quite a memory. Worth revisiting,"

"Speaking of memories, do you remember the time you went after me with your hockey stick?"

"You made fun of my broken incisors," she justified.

That evoked a hearty laugh.

"Ah those days went by in a whim. We were so playful,"

"You were reserved. Like a rock, unyielding, never opening up,"

"It wasn't until Hosse came along that I started conversing more. He has that charm about himself,"

"You and Isabell were always so close. Everyone thought you liked her,"

"She is my best friend. You'd be crazy not to like her. But love is different,"

"How so?"

"Hosse told me about you the very first time he introduced himself. A darling brother you have made. But it wasn't until I felt your love in that gesture, that I started thinking about you,"

"What gesture are you talking about?"

"A game of tag ends when you outdo the last player you are with. On that day, everyone was rambunctiously cheering us on. Still, there was the spirited voice of a girl that resonated with my beat. It was yours. Until then you must have dropped relentless hints, but none involved you calling out my name. The moment I heard you cheer my name I recognized a zest unlike anyone's. Truth be told, in that moment I sealed my heart's beat in your voice. One moment of the unrestrained real you before me was all it took,"

"You never said this before,"

"You never asked. We never had a proper conversation until Hosse's wedding. You assume a lot Charloette. All girls do. Guys have a much simpler heart. We don't forget the first girl who evoked love in us dear,"

"It was me,"

"Who else have I searched for? In every morsel of my fabric, it's you,"

"You've got your way with words, and expressing how you feel. I am touched, Christoff,"

"Glad to hear that,"

"On a serious note, have you considered writing?"

"Not really. But I've got a story in my mind. It's a matter of time and commitment when it comes to penning down one,"

"If you do write one, do so from your heart. Mind convolutes the plot to make it extravagant. Sophistication lies in simplicity of perspective,"

"I'd keep that in mind,"

Without realizing we had conversed our way to the Little Angels.

"Time flies with you by my side,"

"Let's enter in, writer" she winked jovially.

"There you are. Boy, I am glad to see you two," said Mary embracing us.

"It's nice meeting you Grandma," said Charloette.

"Christopher surely did choose an angel," she said endearingly.

"You raised her up. In a way you gave me my angel,"

"I gave you advice. It was you who followed it through. And what a gem you've found,"

All this adulation flustered Charloette a bit. But she maintained her joviality.

"Mary, Christoff said you wanted to talk about something,"

"Yes, I do. Now that you both are together, it's about time,"

"Anything troubling you," I asked noticing the change in her tone.

"No, my dear. On the contrary it's making me nostalgic,"

"What is it?" Charloette asked.

"Follow me into my room," said she leaving us.

Mary lived a simple life. Devoting most of her time to us children and this orphanage. She was a violinist and a music teacher. And she played us rapturous melodies that lightened up our childhood with hope. Her room was a testament to her spirit. She kept it colourful and pristine.

From her closet she took out a small box. It was navy blue in colour with a yellow ribbon.

"Here, open it together," she said handing us her prized possession.

Inside lay a paper-thin gold leaf. It was heart-shaped like an alocasia's and engraved.

"Your Grandpa gave it to me on our wedding," she reminisced.

"There are writings on it," remarked Charloette, "Deft and miniscule,"

"Those are the vows. 7 to be precise," she explained, "Here, take this magnifying glass and read it,"

"1. To cherish life together

2. To be a loyal comrade

3. To be kind and helpful

4. To love wholeheartedly

5. To care unexpectedly

6. To apologize irrationally

7. To hold you dear forever,"

"Your Grandpa always used to say that one set of vows for a lifetime of growing together with you could not suffice. Still, those 7 vows you just read form the foundation of any relationship. Making it last is a serious commitment. For all I know, where there is love, people always find a way to make it work. Love compels them to better themselves for the sake of their beloved,"

"It's a nice present Grandma. You've kept it with care," said I

"And I want you both to have it,"

"Us?"

"Yes. It's a tradition. Consider it a family heirloom and treasure what it says. It was time to pass it down. You two make a lovely couple,"

"Thank you," said Charloette.

"We'll take good care of it like you did,"

"I know you will. That's why I gave it to you," said Mary, "Now, join us for dinner. It's been a long time since we've dined together,"

"The more, the merrier,"

"Food tastes better with loved ones at the table,".

March 29

It had been two days since I started reading this journal Christoff had penned down. He had a talent of expressing himself which reflected in his writings. Succinctly put it was a dive into his past that foreshadowed his present. A story to retell for ages. Nearing the end, I figured out it was incomplete.

Mary's last wish was that I read this. She probably noticed my feelings during my visits to Shaira. Sadly, that guy was ever elusive.

"Christopher is not an easy person to understand," said Mary.

"He keeps himself guarded," I replied.

"The ones who are most reserved turn out to be the most interesting ones. Christopher is astute in observing. He keeps his opinions to himself unless asked for,"

"Was he always like this?"

"Not always. Things happen in life that can harden the most tender of men,"

"Did something terrible happen in his past?" I asked curious.

"Nothing that can be undone," she said with a wry smile.

The next few days I searched for the missing links to his story. As the investigative wing of The Times scourged through numerous files of Riviera, the world summit atop Angel Falls was approaching. Its coverage would soon turn out to be the highlight of my career.

"The March 29 bombings," said one of my colleagues "Of the 7 places blown, one is the Barrows,"

"The year?" I asked.

"2006. You wouldn't know but the Riviera Bombings till date is considered to be the greatest lapse in the intel forces of our country,"

"Was the accused caught?"

"No one took claim for the merciless explosions,"

"Why call it merciless?"

"The places that were targeted are all civil areas,"

I had refrained from sharing details regarding the Barrows with my team. The only leads they had, were the names of Christoff, Charloette, Hosse, and Isabell. Considering the paucity of time, they had done a commendable job.

"Rachel, name out the places,"

"The southern suburbs, Hopewell Hospital, St. John's Cathedral, Metropolitan Square, Gilmore Fountains, and an orphanage,"

"An orphanage?"

"The Little Angels in the east side of Riviera,"

"The casualties?"

"51 people. Including Hosse Hoffman and Charloette Whitman,"

As we delved further, I realized the crux of the matter. Christoff left Shaira in search of the person who committed those said atrocities. His involvement with the Barrows jeopardized the safety of the orphanage's children and his friends. From the facts all this pointed towards one unidentified person who went by the alias of Vega. Christoff held himself accountable for their deaths. When guilt keeps gnawing at your heart, the desire for vengeance inevitably creeps in. Held prisoner in its grip, the best of men have fallen. And I couldn't afford losing him.

"It's that time of the year again," Isen remarked.

"The time it all fell apart," said Jeffrey.

"Christoff really had to make a tough choice. Yet he did unflinchingly,"

"Love gives you that resolve. To defy the entire world,"

"He did it with an unabashed attitude,"

"He surely did Isen. I clearly remember that day. We were in the office at the Barrows. One year had passed since Yorkshire. Work was few and I was literally dozing when the telephone rang. A feminine voice asked for Christoff using the extradition code we were assigned. She sounded desperate. I forwarded the call to him and the next moment we were scurrying towards the exit tunnel as ordered by Christoff. 20 minutes later the bombings took over the news,"

"I have a snippet of that article. The columnists gave in quite a punch,"

"Raining Fire. Hopewell hospital where Isabell's delivery was due lay in ruins. A truck skidded off Metropolitan Square ramming into Hosse's car because of an explosion. Little Angels paid its price for having us. The shelter could be rebuilt. But lives once lost are gone forever. 51 people. It's a heavy toll,"

"That call gave you 10 minutes to stop 7 simultaneous explosions,"

"Lives were indeed saved. But someone has to take the blame for the lapse. John was labelled a traitor. And Christoff didn't agree with us for that,"

"He left Shaira on receiving your letter. What did you write him?"

"Diego Vega has been spotted alongside John. They are after Polaris. The Brethren wants them dead,"

"And he rebelled against you, didn't he?"

"His moral conscience won't let him. You know how he is,"

"Does all of this end well?"

"He is going against the Brethren. It's going to be a carnage if he interferes," said Jeff recollecting his last conversation with Christoff.

"What did you just do?"

"I declared war on them,"

"You out of your mind,"

"On the contrary I finally came back to my senses,"

"Extraditing against us at a world summit will fail,"

"Everyone wins this time. Give my best regards to boss,"

"Why defy the world for him?"

"I owe him my world. That's all the reason I need,"

"If you've decided, then do know this. The moment you step foot on Angel Falls, the Barrows will gun you down. John has his fate sealed in at the summit,"

"Fate lies in the choices we make. You guys made a weak one. It's time to set things right,"

"That will be the death of you,"

"You feel most alive closest to death,"

"Christoff. Consider this again. You do know who's overseeing the coverage of this,"

"Ensuring everyone's safety will be your responsibility,"

"Those are the words he left me with Isen," said Jeff.

"She is weaved into his life's fabric. One way or another their worlds will collide,"

"What choice will she make?"

"He's foreseen that. He knows her. That's why he's so sure,"

"The world's fate will be in balance. Can we leave it to the emotions of one girl?"

"She is one in a millennial girl. Her choice is deserving enough of sealing in everyone's fate,"

A world summit was being organized by the United Nations of the Sovereign. 12 countries were to spearhead this mega event. Its purpose, the launch of global satellite interlink, which when deployed would create a gigantic array of interconnecting digital feed mapping every corner on Earth simultaneously. The data generated would be enormous requiring a mountain of storage and a never before invented cooling system for the quantum level computers. Angel Falls located near the arctic pole was the designated area. Frigid bone numbing air atop this mountain was ideal. The steepest water fall man had known was being used as a coolant for this project titled Polaris.

"They are bringing the entire planet into one screen using holograms," said Rachel.

"Yes, unlike traditional geo-mapping, it's a round the clock surveillance," I replied.

"We'll be there covering at sub-zero temperatures,"

"Bon Appetit, dear. It will be March 29 tomorrow when we land. Get some sleep,"

"So do you, Lisa,"

"Will you be there?" I thought staring at the clouds, "Riviera got decimated because of Polaris. What is in it that made you disappear for 6 years?"

Thoughts darted recklessly before sleep caressed me in its clutch as I watched the setting sun slant into wispy clouds praying for one thing.

"Hope I'll meet you there, Christoff,"

Early morning felt like a wintry night as we stepped down the aircraft. The air was frigid, bereft of any sunlight. Relentless snow-covered peaks showed the hostility of life at the poles.

"6 months of pure winter," said Rachel.

"Do not wander off here. These places hide the most vicious of creatures," I replied

"Wolves and polar bears?"

"You know better to keep yourself away from ferocious animals. I'm talking about that plant over there. A single prick of its thorn can paralyze you. Then there's that thin ice that will send you into freezing waters when you step on it. Life here is about survival,"

"How do you know all of this?" she asked curious.

"I spent a year in Greenland with my mother. She told me about life at the poles,"

"Pretty wise of you to remember it,"

"We'll discuss my travels later," I said looking at my watch, "The summit kicks off in 4 hours. Get the rest of our team,"

"Yup, I'm already on it,"

Our journey to the summit gave us a scenic view of the bewitching Angel Falls. Water gushed down into a cauldron below stirring up heavy mist that enshrouded the foothills into a cloak of invisibility.

"It's so steep," said our cameraman.

"You better not go near it's edge," said the chauffeur.

"A fall down the Angel's is a straightway ticket to icy heavens below," quipped Rachel.

"Appreciate your sense of humour. Do keep it up. For we'll need it as we cover the event in these harsh conditions," I blurted out.

"Suppose someone does fall down, do they survive?" asked our buddy who wanted a close up shot atop the falls.

"It'd be a miracle. And they don't often happen in here. I'd say that person would be a rather lucky bloke," I replied.

"Now that you mentioned it, there's a legend about the Falls," said the native

"A legend. That'd be nice to hear,"

"It is said that a phoenix was once spotted gliding down into its depths. Wings of fire doused in those waters before it re-emerged flaming hot after that cold dive,"

"I thought phoenix arose from its ashes,"

"They do. But it's a metaphor to correlate with. Time is the ash that hides in Angel Falls. When a person willingly jumps down that beast of a waterfall, then his lifespan is dwindled into an ash. And from those ashes, arises life of the person for whom the act was committed for,"

"Only a crazy person would do something so stupid," I commented disapprovingly.

"Such kindred souls do exist, madam. Maybe you'll meet one,"

A gleam showed in the man's eyes as he uttered those words, driving us closer to our fated destination.

"The Summit awaits," Rachel prepped up the atmosphere back to our coverage as we stepped down from our van.

"ID's please," asked the Delta Forces at the checkpoint.

A thorough security scan with frisking was carried out in an immaculate manner. No lapses were allowed knowing all the world dignitaries would be present in one place.

No sooner had we entered the gate than we spotted the British government as the members alighted down from their black SUVs. That was our window of opportunity to get a sneak peak of the forthcoming events.

Together with Rachel and Mark we quickly made our way to the scene and secured an interview with their spokesperson.

"Madam, could you brief us about the launch of this decade long project?" I interviewed.

"Polaris will strengthen the hold of the Sovereign Union over the Asian skies," said Nicola Sedenham who was spearheading this event.

"The Asians seem hesitant about your satellites invading their airspaces,"

"It's a necessary trade-off. For a global satellite interlink it was pivotal,"

"Forgive my intruding but the Brethren King's speech is most awaited after his health scare. Any updates on that," I asked tactfully.

At this she smiled slightly and replied, "Rayman Jr. will indeed speak on behalf of his father. He is a capable businessman and a visionary. His insight over the years made this mega event a reality today,"

With that she re-joined the British convoy cutting short the interview.

"That's the way it's going to be folks," I told my crewmates, "Swift and precise,"

"Gotta get used to it," realised Mark.

"What is the Brethren?," asked my cameraman, "Sounds archaic,"

"The Brethren is the moniker for The World Council headed by the most influential person on earth aptly name King," answered Rachel.

Our crew began surveying the spot for setting up the broadcasting equipment. Strategic locations like the Amphitheatre where Rayman would deliver his public speech were emphasized upon. A strict no interference policy at the banquet hall had been issued. The stunning multi tiered castle had wide battlements overlooking the haunting Angel Falls. Snipers from the keep tower secured the perimeter below while drones kept hovering in the sky providing 360 degree surveillance of the World Summit.

"It will be a grand turn of events should Christoff Myers show up," said Jefferson Spiegel head of security as I stood looking down at the Falls.

"How do you know him?" I asked surprised.

"He's a dear friend of mine. Our intelligence keeps track of our agents. He last met you in Shaira, Miss Lisa Sparks,"

"Then you must know about the March 29 bombings, Mr. Jefferson," I came out upfront.

"I cannot reveal state secrets. But do know this Myers is a wanted man for helping John escape capital punishment,"

"Then is he on the right side or is he a threat to national security?" I didn't hesitate from asking.

"He's a righteous guy to his core. And the only persons you should probably trust are your crewmates and him," he advised before leaving.

His voicial intensity hinted at a terrible turn of events. One he was in charge of preventing.

"Quite a mess your absence has made in everyone's life. A-hole," I thought to myself as his face quaintly visited my memory.

The Tilted Promise

"Everyone's ready for this?" Diego de la Vega asked John Trueman.

"They are prepped up," answered John.

"It's only natural. This mission will be our last,"

"The Barrows are protecting the Brethren at the Summit. We can easily get in. The trick, however is escaping out,"

"Extraction. We will leave that to C.Myers. He's bound to show up considering what's at stake,"

"I have set the EMP charges on our stealth drones," beamed in a cool headed Sahara.

"What about Allie?" asked John.

"She's busy honing her sniping skills,"

It was one crazy plan our team had come up with. Lead by master planner Diego, John would provide the artillery, Sahara the technical prowess and I, Allie Archer would snipe the final blow. No one in entirety knew the exact plan. It was his idea. Choosing only trustworthy friends to prevent inevitable mishap which was looming due to launch of Polaris.

As the four of us huddled close Diego reaffirmed his faith in us, "Our prime job is to get Lisa Sparks to the authentication bay,"

"Thereafter," inquired Allie.

"We'll leave that to Myers," replied John, "Only he knows of the endgame,"

"Where is he now?" Sahara looked pensive.

"He has his own vendetta to handle,"

At this the group expressed uncertainty but Diego provided assurance.

"He will show up. Be vigilant out there," issuing the final command.

"Do you think he can change the fate of the world?" Destiny asked Luck as they watched the scene unfold from afar.

"Your prediction has never been proven wrong," Luck replied.

"Yet he exudes an aura unlike any other. His titanium clad resolve is stone-edged into my memory,"

"Those who love from their soul write their own destiny," Luck remembered.

"They harbour the Twin Phoenix. You know what that means,"

"Time's the ash from which one's life will renew oneself,"

"Eternal bond. A phoenix giving rise to his soulmate from his ashes,"

"Such a steep price one must pay,"

"Togetherness requires sacrifice. Take in our story,"

Luck could change anyone's luck except his. Destiny could predict anyone's fate except hers. The two loved each other but became proud of their ability. Which is why the Creator cast a spell on them. They could always be together but never hold hands. To break that spell they had to find that lucky couple who would live up to the Creator's words-

"When one's true love will overturn Destiny's foretelling of their fate so much so that Luck will get compelled to change Destiny's prediction, that spell would get broken,"

"Centuries passed where Luck tried searching for them. Many came and went by. Even Destiny got disheartened by her own predictions. Truth be told people got accustomed to "I love you" being spoken and expressed so many times, they forgot it's meaning.

Love makes you one with your soulmate. So much so that I becomes you, and love is the only thing reflected in each other's perspectives.

Meanwhile the world's fate had been set into motion.

"Arrowed right into the sweet spot," replied Fred our marksmen.

Sahara immediately fiddled at her laptop over-riding the drones designed by Jeffrey using her own chipset.

"Gained access," she said triumphant, "Looping video feedback,"

"We're secured. Let's roll," said Allie from her backseat.

A red Benz drove up to the entrance guarded by the Delta Squad. The glass window came down to reveal a strikingly attractive woman. Greeting in a serene tone she held out her card.

"The insignia of the Royal Family," verified the guard setting in inevitable commotion. Dressed in red the heiress spoke in majesty and commanded absolute authority.

"Sahara Buergess," said she and instantly the gates flung open. While the Benz drove in, an inaudible sound wave inundated the ears of the Delta Squad members and lulled them into sleep.

"You can take out your earplugs Allie," she replied smiling.

"Playing the Juancos sleeping melody into their ears was ingenious,"

"It was Myer's idea. Now get your disguise. We'll rendezvous at Authentication Bay,"

Sahara was tasked with the most important role. One which would swing the pendulum onto our side.

On the other hand John and I went about commencing the diversion.

"High altitude dives from stratosphere. It's insane," John remarked

"Christoff's ideas are wackier. Believe me," I said in jest

Our camouflage suits were designed to escape radar while slowing down our descent. Meanwhile the EMP would sweep the drones shut.

"On the count of 1,2,3. Fire," The EMP payload came descending down on timer ready to wreck havoc.

"Let's jump,"

An out of the world experience of sky boarding down the altitude with tremendous force was overwhelming. As the drones came into view, the payload fired off the EMP rendering them powerless. They fell like hailstones allowing us to slip below their radar onto the drawbridge.

"Arm yourself up. It's showtime,"

The congregation inside the Amphitheatre Hall eagerly awaited Rayman's speech. His personality, as heard was magnanimous. Walking up the stairs he exuded sheer confidence and began.

"It's a privilege to be spearheading the launch of this decade-long project. Polaris aims to 3d holograph the entire biosphere onto digital displays. Enabling 24*7 surveillance with high precision land mapping, interconnected through satellite web. Such quantum computing generating yottabytes of data required mega storage facilities, and an unprecedented cooling system. Angel Falls at the Northern Pole was the preferred destination and it gives me immense pleasure to inaugurate the launch of the satellites,"

His command over the audience was beyond superb, and it looked that the launch would be successful. But then the unthinkable happened.

The glass windows of the amphitheatre shattered at once before the lights went out. Dark mayhem gripped the summit as the drones crashed into the vicinity, forcing the Delta Squad to quickly assume their defensive position. All exits were secured, and the dignitaries reassured of their safety.

"EMP Resonance," said Jeffrey Spiegel, head of security, "Wear your protective gears. And follow me,"

No sooner the inaugural had turned into a battlefield, for the opposing countries wanted to stop the deployment of Polaris, citing national security. It could literally bring down the communication system of an entire nation with the click of a button, isolating them. And in wartime, communication is the key factor deciding victory.

"John play out Beethoven's Sonata," I asked as drones fell over like raindrops.

The security personnel at the drawbridge, confusingly moved in to surround us as we both lifted our hands and announced with utmost dignity,

"Take us to Rayman," John announced remorseless.

"Look at where you stand," said the Lieutenant, "You have no right to negotiate. Do stop the music,"

"With pleasure," I said as John stopped the classic mp3 player.

Instantly gunshots singed into our ears as Allie took aim from the keep tower. One after another the tranquilized soldier fell onto the ground as we took out the rest of the regiment.

"Nice cue," Allie thought over to herself as her tranquilizer gun combined with the mp3's gunshot proved pivotal. It did alert Jeffrey's squadron to spread out allowing Sahara, who was at the amphitheatre to draw close to Lisa.

"Miss Sparks," Sahara hushed into her ears as she stood in the dark, "Don't shout,"

"I have a message from your friend Christoff Myers,"

His mere mention struck a delicate chord as she asked instinctively, "Where is he?"

"The man you see standing at the podium in darkness. Walk over to him,"

Without questioning any further she did as she was told.

Ascending the flight of steps she realised the familiar figure.

"How are you?" asked Lisa.

"Doing good Miss Sparks," answered a jovial Christoff.

"I thought Rayman Jr. was giving the speech,"

"I'll explain later, but first let's make our exit,"

He removed this cover which was concealing a man-hole that Newman had designed under the podium.

"Stand still," Christoff instructed as the pitch dark frantic atmosphere made for a perfect getaway.

"Climb down Lisa,"

I did as he asked and found myself in an underground exit tunnel.

"Where does it lead to?"

"To the Authentication Bay and out into the arctic lands. Follow me,"

Moving along swiftly we came across a sealed vault with a biometric enabled lock. At this Christoff halted and turned round to face me. It allowed me to catch a proper glimpse of his face. It hand changed drastically. He had grown a thick beard, and sported a pony tail hairstyle. Dressed in his burgundy tuxedo he appeared elegant. So much so I did lose myself for a moment admiring this transformation.

"Lisa," he snapped me into reality, "Listen carefully to what I have to say,"

His voice sounded pensive demanding attention, implying the gravity of our situation.

"Go ahead,"

"This biometric can only be opened by your iris data,"

"What!"

"You aren't adopted. Newman Reeds, the creator of TransformWear, was your father. He invented Polaris alongside Diego de la Vega,"

"How does all of this connect to me?"

"Access the Authentication Bay to find out,"

My iris signature turned the vault open and as we stepped inside, we were greeted by a holographic projection of Newman Reeds standing near the CoreHub.

"Hi there. If you have come this far, you must certainly be my daughter," he said, "Your presence here is going to decide the fate of the world. You see, Polaris is a dual edged sword. In the name of geomapping and connectivity, they have targeted genomic sequence of races. Once the Z-rays emitted by those satellites at their mutation frequency sets in, it can decimate an entire nation into servitude. Those who opposed it were either silenced or their origins erased,"

"That is wrong," I said in anguish.

"It's a projection. He can only say what's pre-recorded," Christoff reminded me.

"The only way to stop this program is via the data drive that I requested Diego to relay to you. Once embedded into the core architecture it would erase the genetic data and Z-ray emission," Newman continued, "Lastly all that remains is you. I have always loved you dearer than my life. You came as a blessing and changed all of our lives,"

With that the projection disappeared leaving me overwhelmed.

Teary eyed I replied, "I don't have any data drive,"

"I know which is why we decided to hard reset the CoreHub using the algorithm developed by our team. The purpose of you coming here was to meet your father,"

"Where do we go from here?"

"You go back to your home in Riviera, while the Barrows realigns with its real purpose,"

"What about you?"

"I go by the alias of Rayman Jr. It took me 6 years to reach this position. The countries at the summit are unaware of our decision to erase the Z-ray emission architecture permanently,"

"Back at Shaira, I should have told you this - "

But before I could speak the woman who had led me to Christoff appeared and announced in affirmative tone.

"Diego and John have secured the premises as planned, you need to get out," said Sahara.

"She's right, we'll talk it out later,"

Meanwhile Sahara accessed the CoreHub and began infiltrating the resources of the World Council to erase all research data of the Z-rays and its deployment,"

"You guys get going, it's gonna take a while,"

"Sure enough,"

Moving forwards Christoff and I made our way out of the bunker towards the exit stairs.

"What about Diego?" I questioned.

"Diego went by the alias of Reaper, was an excellent strategist at the Barrows," I replied, " Having recruited me to aid him internally he went round the world forming alliances to stop Polaris,"

"So these 6 years you've worked with Rayman,"

"He's an ally in the World Council. Because of his support we were able to helm the top brass of this Summit,"

"But the files connect him with Alejandro,"

"The Barrows not withstanding his revolt defamed him, and linked his identity to Alejandro de la Vega's brother who they had assassinated. Despite the chaos, the promised day arrived as planned,"

"What was your plan?"

"You work at the Times, don't you?"

"Yes,"

"Then I have a request," He took a data drive from his sleeve coat and handed it over to me, "This is the twin drive. Keep it with you,"

I did as he asked before he opened the door letting in the Arctic wind shiver us to our core.

"Put this on," said Christoff, "Handing me his overcoat,"

Untucking his shirt and folding up the sleeves, he freed himself from his formal attire and went about his work adeptly.

Back onto the surface, the Angel Falls was heard gushing and swirling in foams.

"It's the closest I have seen this," I remarked.

As we continued progressing forward a chopper came into view. It stood still on the docking area above the steep slope which we were moving towards. Christoff held my hands and led me through.

"Don't step on the mines," he cautioned, "They are concealed in the snow,"

Progressing forward a man was seen awaiting us. Christoff advised me to hold my stance and walked up to him.

"Helinsky,"

"You cannot leave this place, Myers. The Barrows struck a cross deal with me to deliver you to them, "

The two of us stood on a platform covered in snow bordering the precipice. Helinsky had no intention of negotiating, as he quickly pulled out a gun and pointed it towards Lisa.

His fingers were on the trigger before I wrestled it off in a tussle. Burly as he was, his brute strength was countered by direct hits on one's weak spots. Removing his grip, the gun went off in mid-air before falling onto the ground. A heel kick to Helinsky's temple knocked him down but he activated the charge on the platform, setting in the timer.

Lisa on hearing the gunshot had mistakenly stepped onto the twin platform before I could warn her.

"Stay there," I shouted.

The twin charge explosives were pressure mines which when activated gave us 10 seconds to decide each other's fate. Whoever stepped off first would die, deactivating the other. If neither did, both would be blown away.

Knowing the stakes, hesitation was uncalled for to protect the ones dearest to you. In a moment I made up my mind, and relayed in my final command,

"Do it,"

Allie was overseeing this from the mountain slope as she pulled her trigger lodging a bullet right into Helinsky's thigh.

"Curse it," Helinsky screamed in agony.

Nonetheless he got up and tried tackling me down. I somehow managed to hold my ground. But time was ticking. Only two seconds remained. Grabbing him by his neck I stopped his inertia before looking into Lisa's eyes.

Recollecting all moments of a lifetime, I smiled nostalgically and in the blink of an eye plunged myself down the beast of a Fall.

Instantly the explosion set the place ablaze, as we fell down the waterfall.

Shaken as Lisa was by the explosion, she stood up and ran over to the edge trying to make sense of what had happened.

Standing mum she looked below before falling down to her knees, and crying out in remorse.

The man she loved was gone. And the herculean task he left her with changed her entire life.

While she knelt their moaning, a hand reached over to her shoulders.

"You'll catch frostbite crying in the arctic," said the woman.

Blurry through her tears Lisa couldn't make out who she was until she answered herself.

"Allie. My name's Allie Archer. I am one of Christoff's friend," she ascertained, "He tasked me with transporting you back to Riviera,"

"We should search for them," Lisa implored.

"Our crewmates will do that. Your safety is of prime concern for you now possess the complete twin drive,"

"What does it contain?"

"Everything all the governments have ever done throughout the history of human civilisation,"

"But he may be alive. I have to go down there and find him,"

"Please understand. If you truly love him, leave this place at once,"

Her heart didn't want to accept what her mind had seen, yet she boarded the chopper and left Angel Falls peering over the gigantic waterfall into which love had fallen.

Faulted Lines

It was night as the chopper descended onto the Times roof. Pitch black like my soul for light had left alongside him, I stepped down determined to showcase the world the truth of the Brethren.

Walking into the telecast room, I plugged the twin drive in the broadcasting computer, and instructed my team to scourge through the gigantic array of data, compiling the segments of the 24*7 non-stop broadcast which would last for 3 consecutive days.

The hostage situation at the World Summit cleared up as Diego and John showed our telecast of the real plot behind Polaris to all the nations.

"This is what he would have wanted," I pondered sitting morose on a bench in the park.

Our viewership skyrocketed worldwide as governments toppled down, and the world got reformed for good. He had even ensured international amnesty for his colleagues involved in thwarting the World Council's dominion over Earth.

A month went by where the rescue team turned Angel Falls inside out hoping to discover their bodies. Alas! it came to nothing.

Commemorating his memories, a funeral was organised in his hometown at Riviera. It was morning hours when I was visited by August's mother. Trisha looked distraught and August inconsolable.

"First of all forgive me," I said.

"It's not your fault dear. He did that for love," explained Martha.

Tears trickled down August's cheek as he came to terms with the fact of living a life without Christoff.

He once told them that should he die, then Isen be the one, as his dear brother, to say the final words of the ritual at his funeral.

At this Isen's plight exaggerated. He tried not to cry, but failed. And so he cried bitterly. A few minutes passed like this when he made up his mind and got himself up to deliver Christoff's eulogy.

Isabell laid down her bouquet over his tombstone as several questions plundered my sanity. My existence had turned into penance.

I too was grief-stricken and nothing anyone could say could console me.

"Don't do that to yourself, please," said Isabell

Knowing how much he was loved I put my head onto my mother's lap and cried out loud. I cried out all my feelings till none was left.

Still the eulogy remained as I restrained my emotions and carried myself around.

"I stand here as an elder brother," Isen spoke to the congregation, "For all the time I have known Christoff, I found him to be a good person. Sacrifice ain't easy, but love makes it easier. That's what he taught me. To love and only love. May his life forever inspire people to move on no matter what the world throws at you. And at last may you my brother finally rest in peace,"

Everyone paid their condolences and finally it was time to bid goodbye.

And there I stood in front of his tombstone, on which the saying was carved in stone for eternity -"May Spring waltz into your life, like it did it mine,"

Such was fate for when I left the graveyard that lay covered in snow and headed for a new place, a voice called out to me.

"Going somewhere,"

"Yes, a place where I can find solace,"

"Then join me,"

"And where to?"

"To Hewlett," she said handing me her card.

A New Life

9 months have passed since I visited Hewlett. That experience has taught me many things. One of which is very vividly written in the book that I am currently reading.

"Love has sacrifices. But what is that love that doesn't transcend pain, and only lives in the shadows of happiness,"

"Who are we if not humans. Mere creations in this intangible world. Despite walking on fine threads ourselves, we dare to perceive emotions. We dare to love, willing to get entangled in a web with someone else. But how many of us, have the guts to cut all ties off, and let that one person, who means the world to us, depart,"

"Yes, farewells may be unavoidable in these ever-changing seasons of life. Definitely times will come when my voice may not reach you and neither can your eyes find me. But I'll continue to walk by your side no matter what. That's the promise I'll keep,"

"A promise to love you. To be too selfish to share my pain. Too arrogant to be pitied. Too stupid as to make you, who fell in love with me question,

"Why did I fall in love with this idiot?"

These are the words that have conflicted the readers of this story.

Such intense passion, but this book has it's light moments as well. And know what, today I'm visiting the author of this phenomenal sensation "Waltzing Hearts". It has enraptured hearts of millions of people around the world. Some say that it's tragic, others romantic, but as far as I have read, only one word is apt, "It's soulful,"

Right now I'm in the flight and am reading the book that has all the world curious. "Curious" I dare not say anything less. Do you know why? Because

The story's incomplete. The author E.Hugo said in an interview that the story will write itself. It's ending will be known only when time comes.

And today I'm about to document her inspiration for this book. It's going to be fun.

It's evening time when the plane lands in Hewlett. From there on, a cab is kept ready for me which I aboard and drive straight to Hugo's house. Its a simple looking but spacious home. There the valet attends to me, and shows me to the waiting room.

I wait there for an hour then two, but the author doesn't arrive. Ultimately the valet comes in and apologises for the inevitable.

"I'm sorry, but E.Hugo cannot make it here today. Some urgent family matter requires to be dealt with," the valet says.

"That's sad. I wanted to do this interview myself. But never mind....will she be available tomorrow?" I ask.

"Yes....."

"Very well, then tomorrow my assistant will come here and document the interview," I say to the valet and leave the premises.

On the pavement, my car awaits me and I enter in with a sigh.

It's a pity that I must leave Hewlett so soon, for my own company has its Foundation Day tomorrow. And that's very important for the chief Editor.

I fly back to Riviera, the next morning, where a busy day awaits me.

No sooner do I land there than I get engaged in work. The arrangements have been done meticulously. The front office lawn has been decorated beautifully with white drappings, and red roses. The podium lies to the back in the middle of this big lawn. An orchestra has been organised to commemorate this auspicious occasion.

"But one thing's missing," I tell my fellow sub-ordinate.

"Missing? What?" he asks frantically.

"My dear friend. Are you going to attend this event in your night dress?" I say laughing.

"Bugger. My suit, it's with the tailor, I better get it back," he exclaims in surprise and leaves with considerable haste.

His name is James Butler. He's a good friend of mine and a very good person. In fact he's been here in the office since late night. So his messed up condition. And as for the pyjamas, his house is nearby, so that ain't to be worried about.

The event starts rolling by mid-afternoon when the orchestra plays us a warming tune. Its beats are subtle and random, but there's a faint glint of hope in them. There in the black suit, a man orchestrates the choir with great nimbleness and deft touch. He's so engrossed in his work that he never for once takes his eyes off from the choir.

Ten minutes or so pass by and the music finally reaches its concluding part. I await for it to end but that's when my cell phone rings and I have to leave the premises to attend the call.

"Yes," I say picking up the call.

"Sorry mam, but I couldn't get an interview with the author," says my co-worker.

At this I feel a bit disappointed and end the call by saying, "It's okay, you can come back,"

Thereafter I re-enter the premises and resume my seat only to find everyone clapping there in applause.

"Did I miss anything?" I ask my colleague.

"Yes. The ending of the music was superb...That man orchestrated it flawlessly," she says.

I look around towards the stage but sadly the choir has already left, and only a lady stands there thanking the crowd for their appreciation.

A few minutes pass by before my own turn comes. I ascend up the steps and stand on the podium. There, after taking a deep breath, I give my formal speech congratulating everybody and then the celebrations kick in. A huge buffet of various cuisines has been arranged on the lawn. There the people sit in their chairs around the roundtable, and enjoy a hearty meal.

As for me, I stand at a corner near a yew tree and watch this happy congregation.

While I am smiling, a familiar hand enclasps me from my back, and a voice whispers into my ear, "How are you, beautiful?"

The instant I hear that, I turn round, and give a cry of surprise and excitement.

"Adam, you here...I thought you weren't back from your trip," I say hugging him.

"Well I couldn't stay away from you this long," he says in his charming manner.

"Really," I take a few steps back and look at his eyes, "Still flirting,"

"Well I do have a right to do that," he replies.

"Yes you do. Do you wanna go someplace else?" I ask him.

"Yes. Let's go to a restaurant and catch up with all our news,"

Adam is the person who made me live life again. He got to know me and sooner than I could know, I had started smiling again. We dated for 7 months or so before he proposed to me. Well what more can I say. He's my fiancée.

A Summer Meeting

"This weekend, huh," I say pondering as we sit inside a restaurant.

"Yes," he says to me, "All the arrangements have been done. However, it needs your approval,"

"...Uh huh....." I knowingly delay my answer.

"Take all the time you can," he says teasing me, "But I ain't leaving empty handed,"

At this, I give a laugh and say, "Very well then. So Sunday it is,"

"Yup,"

"But do wear something nice, otherwise I'll run away from the altar," I taunt him.

"I won't let you. Not when I see you dazzling in that white gown," he replies with humour.

We both share our moments, and it turns out to be a beautiful day. We do some touring around the city, deciding what and what not to do on the marriage day. The light talks, good food, and the free spirit of travel, make our little journey very bright.

And so in the coming few days, we get settled into our work life always awaiting the weekend.

If anyone, at this moment were to ask me, about my feelings , I could confidently say that

"Yes I have moved on in life. Moved on from Christoff. And I'm happy,"

However what power does a meagre human have over the future, and so it was during the week before the engagement that destiny spun its wheel, and the world came crashing down onto me.

My assistant hadn't been able to meet E.Hugo. Hence there had been no interview. But this Friday, I had received a call from the author herself, who invited me to come down to Hewlett. She wanted to make up for her inadvertent delays.

I had accepted her invitation and had gone to her place the same day, and this was our interview.

The lady was middle-aged, but looked very pretty. She had an attractive demeanour, and spoke with elegance.

"I'm sorry for the frequent delays, you had to endure. It's just that a family matter required early attention,"

"I understand. So Mrs. Hugo, what was the inspiration of your book?"

"My dear, Waltzing Hearts is an actual story. It's written from a person's own memoirs,"

"Really.... But then why didn't you finish it?" I asked curious

"Because it ain't my story. The persons you have read in this book, they exist. And right as we are talking, they are out there in the real world. And it is my belief, that those two star-crossed lovers are bound to meet. But when will that happen, that only fate can decide.... You see, I'm just a conveyor"

"Okay....But in your story the boy loves the girl, then why doesn't he tell her?"

"That I am afraid I cannot disclose. I promised that person to withhold the secret. I hope you understand,"

"Okay Mrs. Hugo. That should do just fine," I said rising up, "Thank you for lending us the time,"

"The pleasure's mine," she shook my hands after which I left her home.

It was late afternoon, and a light breeze had enveloped the city in its arms. The sky looked cloudless, illuminated by the vivid stars and the shining moon. I was driving home from the interview, along the Hawking Hills, and was descending down the slope towards the intersection that lay a bit ahead. The road was clear, and as far as I could see there was no trouble. But then it happened.

All of a sudden something jumped in front of my car, and I pulled at my brakes with all my might. A squeaking sound erupted the air around and the car stopped. I stepped down immediately, opening the door, and rushed towards the front.

There a familiar creature greeted me. Although it had been a long time since I had seen her, I could still recognise Luce and she was unhurt, or rather so excited that she couldn't stop wagging her tail. She jumped on to me and we fell tumbling down onto the pavement beside the grass.

She kept licking my face and I couldn't stop her. Then a feminine voice rushed in and said, "Are you alright?"

I looked up and saw a young lady standing beside us.

"Yes, I'm okay," I said pulling myself up.

"I'm so sorry. She pulled herself from my grip and ran towards the car,"

"Never mind. But where did you find this spaniel?"

"I didn't find Luce. A person gave it to me to take care of it. By the way why was she licking you? Do you know her?"

"Yes, she belonged to one of my friends,"

"....Wait, are you a friend of Isen Hughes," she asked curious.

"Yes, I'm Lisa,"

"You... are... Lisa Sparks," she exclaimed in surprise.

"Yes," I said patting Luce's head, "but who are you?"

"I am Evelyn. Evelyn Hugo,"

That name struck a chord in memory.

"Wait. You are E.Hugo. But I just met the lady back at her home," I said puzzled.

" That is my assistant. You see, I don't fare well in interviews so she does those for me,"

"Evelyn...," I asked, "Do you happen to know August?"

"Yes," she said in delight ,"Has he come here too?"

"No. But I thought Isen was looking after Luce,"

"Isen, mam, is the one who adopted me,"

"He's married?"

"Yes...why don't you come with us to our home?"

"Sorry I can't. I must leave,"

"Please," she insisted and Luce too tugged at my dress.

"Okay. Hop in the backseat," I told them and off we were.

"So we are returning to that same home I guess," I asked Eve.

"Nope. That's just a feint office," she said, "I live somewhere else. I'll show you the place..... I am sure mother and father will be glad to see you,"

As I was driving, we chatted about many things. One of which was this,

"You are so young. How did you write the story?" I asked.

"I bet that my assistant told you that it was real," she said.

"But....how can such thing be real. I mean why would that person in that story let go of her love,"

"Maybe it's because he loves her, that he doesn't want her to be with him," she said in a solemn voice.

Season of Fall

I drove through a series of streets before we stood in front of a pretty home. As we entered in a sweet fragrance emanated and I said,

"I bet your mother keeps this house so neat and clean,"

"Yes..... There she is. Mummy look who's here?" said Eve.

A pretty lady came out from the kitchen and greeted me.

"You, a friend of Isen?" she asked surprised.

"Yes,"

"Wonderful, take a seat," she said pointing towards the sofa.

She brought me a cup of tea and we began talking.

"So when did you marry Isen?" I asked her.

"4 years ago. We met here in Hewlett and then fell in love,"

"That's sweet," I said with a smile.

She received the compliment with grace and said hesitating

"You know dear, Isen narrated the story to Eve and she liked it so much that she penned it down. Her work got recognised and she became a prominent writer. Then she came here to Hewlett and settled in,"

"What about Shaira?" I asked.

"After Christoff's departure Isen and I moved in here. We occasionally do visit there. Isen is so fond of those kids you know,"

"What is Isen doing now?"

"He is working at the docks,"

"That's nice,"

"So are you staying here in town?"

"No, I got to leave for my wedding. It's in a week,"

"That is nice to hear," she said with reservedness as Eve withdrew into her room.

Our meeting was cut short as my secretary called informing me about my imminent flight schedule to Riviera.

"Sorry, I'm leaving in such a haste,"

"It's alright. Do give us a ring when you are here again,"

"Sure will,"

I left Isen's home undecided. Having gone there reformed and happy, I now returned here conflicted for Christoff's name had sprung up in my life again. That week proved to be the longest debacle in my mind. Nonetheless I kept verve.

Pretty soon the wedding day arrived. And I found myself sitting in front of the mirror, as my mother decored me.

Dressed in a white gown, with my hair hanging down in curls and a red rose crowning my temple hair, I looked pretty. But my face had lost all its smile.

My logic didn't work anymore. I had no words to describe how I felt.

"You look like an angel, Lisa," said my mother.

I didn't reply feeling numb.

Just then the door bell rang and what followed next change my entire story.

"She's getting married today," Destiny told Luck.

"There's nothing that we can do," Luck replied.

"Yet the love in her heart embers in hope," intervened the Creator, "which is why I have a simple task for you Luck -

Go down to that intersection and say a simple left.

"A simple left will turn everything right?"

"Yes it will,"

And so Luck disguised himself as a lost traveller and waited to carry out the Creator's instruction.

A blue car driven by a middle aged woman stopped before a signboard near which he stood.

"Mister, can you tell me where the Aurora Palace is," asked a feminine voice.

"Sure, take a left here, and you'll find it down the road,"

"Thanks," replied the lady before leaving.

"Now where does that road lead her to," Luck pondered.

The blue car halted before the entrance of the wedding venue, as the woman held her gift and bouquet in her hands and walked in to meet the bride.

"Excuse me, could you tell me where the brides room is?" she asked a little girl.

"Right towards the left hand corridor," she replied in a sweet voice.

The woman's footsteps signalled a change in tide as she knocked on the door.

My mother opened it and received in the bouquet with utmost civility before the woman asked for the bride.

"She's in here," replied the mother.

I turned round to meet that voice which would change our universe.

"Charloette," the woman exclaimed in surprise, "My God. It's indeed you,"

Taken aback by the addressal of my name, I appeared perplexed.

Nonetheless she continued, "Gosh. Adam is marrying you. That's superb,"

At that moment. I really wasn't so sure about that. I needed clarity as my mother appeared pensive, "My name's Lisa. Lisa Sparks. You must have mistaken me for another person,"

At this the woman replied, "Definitely not. You were the first person who had a Greek name tattooed onto the back of your waist. I clearly remember you. Don't you recollect?"

Her narrative reminded me of Charloette's tattoo from Christoff's diary before I turned over to my mother for an explanation. Only she could clarify this mess.

Sitting on a chair to soothe her nerves, she drank a glass of water and said in a definitive tone, "I feared this day might come. But before I reveal anything, promise me you would keep calm,"

"I do,"

"Very well then. Your real name is Charloette Whitman. You were involved in an accident several years back after which you suffered from retrograde amnesia. Back at that time you were engaged to Christopher Myers,"

At this she paused, let out a tear and continued, "His occupation put your life in jeopardy because of which I made him leave from your life. All your previous history was erased and you were given a new name of Lisa Sparks,"

"But somehow I stumbled upon him in Shaira. His grandmother sent me his diary. In it, Charloette is his love interest. It is she who has the Greek tattoo," I asked vehemently.

"She was the one who relayed you that diary through August. Seeing you develop feelings for him again made her do so,"

"What about the tattoo?"

"I had it removed through laser after that accident,"

"Then the girl at Charring Cross was me,"

"Right dear. Christopher and you were childhood friends. While you left for foreign education, he found work at the Barrows. On your return, those feelings you had for each other got rekindled. But the incident at the Charring Cross led to the March 29 bombings in Riviera. Seeing this, I considered it best for you to abandon Christopher,"

"Why did you do all of this?"

"It's because I love you. I want a bright secure future for you,"

"Even if it comes at the cost of compromising love,"

"Know this for a mother her daughter's the topmost priority,"

This conversation with my mother unsettled my will. Never before had I felt my identity being torn apart only to find the man I love, love me back. My heart couldn't accept his fall, and today I yearned for his touch.

How could I move forward knowing what he did, was out of love for me.

Winter Frost

The bridesmaid follows me at the back as I advance down the red carpet. I am looking onwards for sure, but not where Adam is standing. For my past is rekindling in front of my eyes. With every step I take, "his" face invades my mind. Those words, those moments I spent with him, rage a storm inside me.

At last I make it to the altar where the priest says the hymn and then we begin to exchange our vows.

It is my turn now, but I hardly have the voice, and it's breaking into a sob. My eyes can't hold back the tears anymore, yet I try my best.

"I....take.....this vow....," I stutter.

Adam realises I'm crying and everyone is looking on to me. He interrupts in between.

"Padre, can I have a moment with her," he asks him.

Then he holds me by the hand and then takes me by the backstage towards a house. As we leave, people whisper their confusion, and some even try calling us back. However Adam listens to no one.

Opening the door he leads me in, and then closes it...

"......You're crying Lisa. What's the matter?" he asks in a tender voice

"It's Christoff...." I say in a broken voice and tell him everything.

He listens intently as he always does, and when I'm finished he only asks one thing.

"Do you love him?"

"...Yes,"

"Then let's leave," he says.

"But the people.." I ask.

"The people....They'll talk about it for a while and forget. What matters is what you believe in?" He says assertively.

He then holds my hand and leads me outside by the back door where his car is.

"Get inside, quickly," he says, "We are visiting Hewlett,"

And so I do, and we both depart from the wedding leaving the audience baffled and whimpering.

After a long journey we finally arrive in Hewlett. Adam drives the car up the Hawking Hills while I simply stare outside the window pane. Dusk has fallen heavily and the sky never appeared more conflicted. It is an inexplicable hue of red and orange.

Stopping his car before the willow gate, we walk up the gravel lined cobble path and would have entered Isen's home if not for the intense music that filled the air with unseen sadness.

I walk towards my right, in the direction of the backyard with Adam following me and see Evelyn standing on a raised platform, orchestrating a group of students, each of them seated on a small black desk, playing a violin.

It seems a spectacle in itself. The lights that decorate the yew tree shine brilliantly and the music seethes right into your heart. It tells a story of pain, yet the subtle beats keep reigniting your hopes.

She notices me standing near the wall and stops midway. Her eyes turn sorrowful and she asks a fellow student to continue orchestrating.

Walking up to me in a gentle stride, she stands in front.

"Lisa....Glad to see you, here. Please come inside," she says and guides us in.

There we sit on the twin sofa with Evelyn facing us.

"Father's away on a trip....." she says but I interrupt her

"Don't pretend anymore?" I say solemnly.

"Pretend?" she acts innocent.

"Yes...my mother has told me everything,"

Those words finally break her will as she closes her eyes and tries to compose herself

"Charloette right," Evelyn finally addresses.

"If you can see us, then you must realise that we have just crashed our own wedding so that Lisa here can see Christoff. Please tell us the truth," says Adam .

"Okay...but first forgive me for holding back," she says.

"I understand why you did it," I reply consoling her.

"Frankly speaking I don't know whether Christoff is alive or not. But I do have this notepad of my father's in which he scribbled a note in his handwriting -

"I am the luckiest person in the world. There are people who care for me. And there is Charloette who cares too much. She has a life ahead and I won't stand there as an obstacle,"

"That sounds just like him," I told her.

"So what are you gonna do?" she asked us

"We don't know," added Adam,"I mean he could be anywhere in this world. We thought you'd know where he is?"

"No I don't," she replied, "He's never contacted us,"

She's telling the truth and there's no more information that we can get there

We thank her for her assistance and leave Hewlett, the same way we had come. Clueless.

However my wish to see him, doesn't flicker a bit. I'm confident that he's alive and I'll find him. There has to be a reason why the tattooist intervened into our wedding.

A Dead End

We travelled to Shaira after we had left Hewlett. There we tried to gather as much as we could about Christoff, but sadly no one had heard of him since.

With no apparent leads, we were forced to return to Riviera.

A week had passed since then, where I had followed every trail that I got about him. But they all turned out to be mere speculation.

With every passing moment, my hopes which were once so strong, were diminishing. I couldn't get myself to focus on my work. Every time I was alone, his face kept darting in front of me. But when I tried to reach him, it withered away like thawing snow.

And so my life turned miserable and winter seemed eternal.

It was a Sunday evening while I lay on the sofa reading Christoff's last words that Evelyn had quoted in her book.

"I'm too selfish to share my pain,"

"Yes you are,"

"I'm too arrogant to be pitied,"

"I know that,"

"Too stupid to make the girl who fell in love with me wonder, "Why did I fall in love with this idiot?""

"But this is were you are wrong. You are stupid for sure. But how could I have not fallen in love with you? You are my life, Christoff. I'm incomplete without you. Please come back,"

"Please...."

I keep crying before I fall asleep sobbing.

Heartbeats

A cell phone rings in a bar at Curacao as men keep gulping down vodka shots down their throats. Folks keep grooving to Caribbean music as a melancholic figure sits round the corner. Her mesh knit cardigan hangs untied over her smock white top and floral embroidered jean shorts while her wet skin keeps glistening in dim light.

"Went up for a late night swim," says Quentin joining in a chair beside her.

"Most are up and celebrating, yet the damsel amongst us is morose. Must have been tough to face loneliness,"

"On the contrary I found someone who could look at me as the woman I am,"

"He's a nice chap," he concurred, "It's a bundle of joy when he's around,"

"Surely is,"

"Wanna go and meet him," suggested Quin.

"Yeah. Let's join our group,"

Walking out the bar, Allison surely made heads turn, as we exited on to the beach.

"You'd melt the ice on any man," he complemented, "Wonder why you were sitting in there glum?"

"Couldn't find one worth melting for," she cheeked in a smile.

Walking on the cold sand as it caressed through our bare feet felt livelier than the festivity inside. Such a magical night couldn't be missed upon. Full moon against the backdrop of starry skies with a gentle sea breeze unfurling your hair, made you long. Long for a companion to share your heart with and who better than our soulful group which lay huddled round the bonfire.

Joining in their lively banter Quin took his spot beside Nora while Joyce sat next to Diego.

"It's a miracle that all of us are alive," said Joyce.

"The man extracting us wouldn't leave a soul behind," remarked Diego

"It's a mission I certainly wouldn't want to repeat," joined in Jeffrey with the drinks.

"You bet that right," said Stephen, "I mean that crazy son of a gun fell down Angel Falls to come out unscathed,"

"And he saved Yuvisko," added Cara.

"I still keep wondering how'd he do that?" asked Alice.

"Uh huh," Quin sought attention, "Allow me to explain,"

"He slowed himself down the falls, courtesy of Jeffrey's grapple hook invention. Coupled with the charged soles of his shoes Christoff applied updraft inside the electromagnetic field I had applied from below using the circular discs floating on the water. Nonetheless grabbing hold of Yuvisko complicated matter, as they fell through the surface with considerable speed. The rest of the escape was through the underground cavern system Jeffrey had mapped out for us. Despite those safety measures it took them a month to recover from those broken ribs. Boy did luck shine on us on that one,"

"It so rarely does in such situations. Gotta give Jeff the credit," said Diego giving Jeff's hand a firm shake.

Alice too sat amongst us quipping up stories of her yesteryears. Everyone sitting in there had a history, a story to tell, yet the one whose story really interested me was amiss, indicated by the vacant spot between Jeffrey and Evans.

"Looking for Christoff," said Stephen laying nestled with Cara.

"Yes,"

"He's on the pier," replied Zico charring in the marshmallows as a delectable aura filled our senses with sweet pleasure.

Glancing around I noticed a familiar figure sitting on the docks. Getting myself up I took leave of the group and made my way across to the wooden pier. I tried my best to approach as steadily as I could, but his senses were sharp. He instantly recognised my nimble footsteps and turned towards me.

"Archer, what brings you here?" said Christoff.

"I could ask the same to you," I replied

"It's the sea waves colliding against the rocks. They remind me of a certain somebody,"

"The lady at the Angel Falls, I presume," said I sitting on the dockside overhanging my legs like he did.

"Her name's Charloette," he replied nostalgic.

"Must have been a special woman,"

"You couldn't even imagine how much,"

"Actually I can. When it compels you to take that fall, it must have been a passionate love, true enough to die for,"

"Good inference you make,"

"So what happened?"

"It's a long story,"

"Hey it's New Year's Eve. We've got plenty of time. Wanna share it on that loneliness you harbour?"

"What makes you interested?"

"Truly speaking I'd like to know the boy inside the man,"

"He's a reserved guy for most part,"

"She's a live wire of a girl. Sexy isn't hot enough to describe that sparkling heart. She be the allegiance pledged onto my soul," I quoted from his work.

"You read the draft,"

"I'd like to know her backstory,"

Christoff at first appeared reluctant but as he continued his mesmerising story fascinated me to my bones.

"Charloette and I were childhood friends. We grew up together at the Little Angels until she got adopted at the tender age of seven while I kept looking after the daily chores of the orphanage. It was a summer meeting while I was working at the Barrows that our relationship got rekindled. We clicked off right from where we had left, but as fate would have it, the incident at Charring Cross forced us apart. It's repercussions were far reaching.

Joyce Scarlett, aid to Diego de la Vega had been captured and kept in remand at the Barrows. On a sultry afternoon, my colleague Jeff received an anonymous call requesting my immediate attention. It was the voice of John. He tipped me off about the imminent explosions that were about to occur.

"Jeff call our agents stationed at the Southern suburbs and tell them to vacate the parking lot near the Prideaux Cafe," I swiftly engaged my intel to vacate the bombing premises.

"St. John's Cathedral and Gilmore fountains followed suit, as the contingency team evacuated all people from there,"

Now all this were co-ordinated on telephone calls. We had to make it appear that we were on the losing side. Instead of defusing the explosives, we let them off, securing the lives of the citizens.

Next was Hopewell Hospital. I called my friend Nicholas who in turn helped in evacuating the hospital via the city's underground tunnel system. It proved difficult. Nonetheless with the help of Trisha and their medical personnel, it was done in ample time.

St. John's cathedral and the Little Angels were looked after by John himself. It did help me out considering the paucity of time as Jeffrey evacuated the Barrows alongside Joyce.

The 10 minutes leverage proved pivotal. Yet the incident at Metropolitan square changed our lives. A truck was overtaking a car at the crossway when the explosive set off, as the rear end of the vehicle crashed against the bonnet. The driver wearing his seatbelt was bruised and bloodied. So was the woman sitting in his side seat. That was the setback of my life.

I reached their way too late with rain pouring down as blood trickled down onto the roadside. The emergency ambulance stretchered off the victims as I caught their glimpse. Falling onto my knees, I looked on as an injured Charloette and my pal Hosse were rushed to the nearest hospital.

"It happened because of her involvement with you," Charloette's mother angrily put the onus onto me. However, I stood their numb awaiting news from the operation theatre. After an arduous night, did the morning bring some sliver of good news.

"Hosse has slipped into coma," said the doctor, "Meanwhile Charloette's head injury in the pre-frontal cortex has kept her unconscious. Their vitals have been stabilised. The bleeding arrested. Now all that remains is to give them the time to recuperate,"

Charloette regained her consciousness after an interval of 18 days. Fragile and weak she couldn't remember her name and identity.

"I cannot assure you that the memory would return. It's retrograde amnesia. Sometimes people never regain them back,"

Her mother considered it apt to shift her to a renowned hospital as we sat there discussing.

"You sure you want to do this," she asked me.

"Yes. Take her away," I said firm and hollow.

She got her new identity as Lisa Sparks, as the Barrows erased all memories of her previous life. The tattoo got erased and I disappeared from her life.

The aftermath on the news read 51 lives were lost to hide the cover-up of the identity change and ensure the safety of the group. With the orphanage destroyed we looked for a safe haven. Nicholas helped out in shifting us to Shaira, while Hosse was relocated to a town hospital, allowing Isabell to visit him on a regular basis.

My guilt forced me to resign from the Barrows, and seclude myself awaiting intel of the mastermind. As was tradition, John was disavowed, and made the scapegoat for the biggest security lapse in Riviera.

I finished a piece of the narrative while Allie listened intently. Pausing midway I turned to look at her face shimmering against the moonlight as she held my hand and consoled me.

"Hasn't Hosse recovered from coma?" she asked.

"No," said I, "Isabell stays in touch updating me about his health,"

"She's a strong woman,"

"Endurance is a mighty calibre she has mastered," I agreed.

"What about Charloette?"

"Charloette ran into me in Shaira, as you must have read from the story. We parted on a friendly term during that visit where she remained unaware of her identity. Her memory hadn't recovered. Yet destiny planned otherwise at Angel Falls,"

"In your story Joyce is played out as an antagonist?"

"The real antagonist was the Brethren's idea of deploying Polaris. It would have enslaved mankind. She helped us, out of her love for Diego, as she relayed me the pen drive when she kissed me at the Hogan factory,"

"Is it the same data drive that you had Hosse relay to Isabell at Avenue Falls?"

"It contains Charloette's memories. But it's encrypted. It's password known only to Hosse,"

"Is that the reason why you planned your escapade at Angel Falls?"

"Charloette has every right to move on in life. I won't stand before her as an obstacle,"

The night turned colder on the pier as Allie too opened up about herself.

"I know how you feel," said she.

"Ever since Max passed away I have lived a vagabond life. That was until you recruited me for the Polaris project,"

"Why did you agree?"

"To find the lady inside the woman I have become is a rare insight for a man to possess," Allie broke her silence, "Beneath your coarse pretence I found a genuine companion,"

"Thanks for that,"

"You know, at first I wondered who would let a guy like you slip away?" she said to me, "But now I realise it wasn't her fault,"

"Charloette's a gem of a woman. And the heart wants what it wants. Can't have any control over its beat now,"

"You are a frank guy, Christopher,"

"And you a great woman,"

Interlude

It's Monday morning when I wake up to the sound of an alarm. Getting on my feet, I try my best to feel optimistic. To convince myself, "Yes, today is the lucky day. The day when I'll meet him,"

Thereafter I make a meagre breakfast and after eating, I leave for the office in my car.

It's only an hour's drive before I find myself back in my cabin.

But instead of working I simply stand there near the glass and keep staring at the skylines.

While I stand there motionless, a knock resounds at the door, and I turn round to find James, my assistant, entering in.

He takes a seat behind the desk, and shows me the documents. I try my best to analyse them, but that's when he asks me the strangest question-

"How do you know this guy?" he says picking Christoff's picture from my desk.

"Do you know him?" I ask eager halting midway.

"Yes. You see my wife who suffers from Addison's disease, once visited Yorkshire hospital during a trip when her health worsened, it was then that I ran into this man,"

"When was this?" I sprang up eagerly.

"About 4 months ago," came in his reply.

At this a spark renewed in me as I spoke with vigour.

"Can you share me the location of the hospital?"

No sooner did he did, I embarked on my homecoming journey.

"Christoff," said Isabell over the cell phone, "Hosse's finger, they moved today,"

"He's regaining consciousness. That is wonderful news," he replied.

"I have called the doctors, they are ascertaining his recovery,"

"Anyone else there with you?"

"No. It's just me out here,"

"I'll inform Trisha and our friends. You stay there with him,"

Isabell almost broke into a sob for Hosse had opened his eyes.

"Oh my God! He's awake," Isabell cried out in happiness.

Even I couldn't hold back my emotions. The long years of wait had extracted a heavy toll on so many of us. Falling down on my knees, I was free from regret as tears of happiness came out in nostalgia.

"Isa," Hosse spoke feebly.

"You were in a coma for a long time,"

"It's nice to see you crying, every now and then,"

"You have no idea how badly I want to slap you, for making me wait so long,"

"You can do that honey, anytime,"

Hosse had kept his sense of humour as he observantly asked, "Who were you talking to on the cell phone?"

"Who else but your brother Christoff!"

"How's that buster doing?"

"A lot has happened. I'll help you catch up. Rest for now,"

They say miracles don't just happen. It takes the coming together of the entire universe to make the impossible possible. Such was the story and the circumstances that led Charloette to the hospital where Hosse had reawakened.

On entering in, she asked out to the receptionist, holding out Christoff's picture.

"Miss, do you recognise this person, he visited here a couple of months back?"

"The lady looked at it for a minute before recalling her conversation with Christoff,"

"Yes he did,"

"Could you tell me who he was visiting?"

"The hospital doesn't allow sharing of patient details, madam,"

"Please, it's an urgent matter," she requested over and over again until she relented.

"It's a man by the name of Hosse Jean Hoffman. He's in room 306,"

She made her way up the stairs before coming to an abrupt halt on seeing Isabell standing outside the door.

"Charloette what are you doing here?" inquired Isa.

"Christoff he's alive isn't he?" she spoke outright.

"He is," she confessed.

"Why hide it when I asked you the first time?"

"It's because you guys have a forgotten history,"

The team of doctors and nurses interrupted our conversation as they talked over with Isabell regarding Hosse's health.

"He's an optimistic person. Should recover just fine. Please ensure he doesn't undergo any emotional duress," said the lead doctor.

Hearing this Charloette calmed down, as Isabell led her inside the room where her husband was sleeping.

Charloette was seeing Hosse for the first time since that accident. It was only natural she didn't recognise his brother.

"Charl, where's Christoff?" asked Hosse.

"She can't remember you," Isabell explained.

"The baby?" Hosse expressed his concern.

"She didn't survive the crash," Isabell narrated the sad turn of events in our life.

Those words shocked the two of them. Hosse couldn't believe the state in which his friends were, Charloette on the other hand was crying out bitterly as she now understood the reason for Christoff's disappearance from her life.

"Christoff and Charloette. The two of you, were engaged at that time. My delivery was due in Hopewell hospital for which the two of you were visiting," said Isabell, "Charloette herself was with a baby for two months. It was then the unfortunate event occurred. Both of you were rushed to the nearest hospital. You slipped into coma while Charloette's baby was declared dead on arrival. With your memories gone, Christoff's guilt made him erase all his memories from your life and depart. Your mother was central to this decision,"

Isabell's narrative shook Charloette to her core while Hosse tried to piece the end of the puzzle in his head.

"Isa, back at Avenue Falls I did slip one into your coat pocket. Do you still have that dress with you?" asked Hosse.

"I did find one and kept it at home. It was encrypted with a password," replied Isabell.

"As far as I can recollect Charloette was with a baby," Hosse revealed, "Who was it that told you about the death of the girl,"

"It was Charloette's mother," said Isa.

"Anyone else who was there at that time with you," Hosse asked Isabell

"All of our friends had gathered at the hospital. Maybe they would know,"

"My condition won't let me leave, but if you could ask someone to bring that data drive Charloette here might be able to regain her memories back,"

Realising the gravity of the situation, Isa immediately dialled Trisha's number and requested her to bring the data drive to Yorkshire.

"I'm on my way," asserted Trisha

The wait for her arrival was tense. Isa was confused, Charloette lay bewildered, while Hosse kept calm. After an arduous two hour wait, did the door flung open, as Trisha entered in.

Our expectant gazes must have startled her, but she kept cool and answered -

"I brought the data drive you had asked for. Here take this,"

Taking out the laptop from his bag, Hosse turned it on before plugging in the data drive and decrypting it with Christoff's password which he had by hearted.

"I believe you have the right to know of this first," said Hosse handing over the computer to Charloette.

Memories Rekindled

The first rays of the morning sun graced onto my face as I found myself leaning on Christoff's shoulders. He was still awake staring at the valley that stood outside. Isen, on other hand, was nowhere to be seen.

I tilted my head sideward and that caught his attention.

"Good morning," he greeted with a smile.

"That smile looks good on you," I replied.

"Sure it does. Here take this," he said handing me a cup

"Latte. Didn't know they served these on trains?" I said surprised.

"Nope, it's from the station's café. We are now at Tiara. Isen's out to stretch his legs. It's a twenty minute stop,"

"Well then let's step out and join him," I replied and pulled Christoff out with me.

As we walked on the platform, the morning breeze felt soothing. The backdrop of the red sky overhanging the rugged hill tops added a rustic charm to this much lonely station. Nevertheless my friend stayed aloof.

"Thank you for coming," I whispered in my mind looking at him.

But somehow the very next moment as I was taking a sip of the latte, he halted and turned towards me saying,

"Did you say anything?"

That gesture caught me unaware and with the cup still in my mouth, I just gazed at those curious eyes of his. For a moment I didn't know how to respond but as he snapped his fingers in front of my face, I quickly gulped down the sip and stupidly answered,

"You some kind of telepath"

"Crap what did I say," I scolded myself as an afterthought.

Christoff's reaction, however was one of laughter. He quickly took a step back and snapped a pic with his phone.

"That'll go down the frame" he commented mischievously.

"What's so funny?" I asked haughtily.

"That moustache suits you, Watson," he chuckled back.

"Whoops," I pondered as a bolt had struck me. Still I was quick to respond by licking the foam in.

"Show it to me," I commanded but Christoff was already off.

The moment it appeared to me, I started chasing him.

"Christoff you baghole, give it to me," I cursed while running.

"Nah I'll be posting it on Foolsbook," he taunted looking back.

A few distance ahead Isen was standing drinking coffee as Christoff went round his back.

"Mate, what's wrong?" Isen said trying to look back at him.

"Stand still Isen," said an animated Christoff

holding him by his shoulders.

"Charloette?" Isen asked puzzled as I rushed towards him.

"Stay out of this Isen," I retorted.

"Whoah," he replied stretching his arm out, shielding Christoff, as I tried to go round him.

"I don't know what's happening. But this isn't the way two adults behave," he answered.

"Tell that to yourself when you're not sober," I joustled back.

"Yeah, him being sober. That's a permanently temporary thing" Christoff teased as he kept dangling his phone behind Isen's back flaunting my moustached picture.

That comment of his evidently piqued Isen and he thus decided to stop playing the role of the wise middleman.

"Give it to me," I replied pouncing.

And the very next moment, Isen stepped out between us, while I came tumbling down on top of Christoff as he cushioned me from the fall.

"Whew! Would have been a waste of some damn fine coffee" said Isen drinking a sip and leaving us down on the platform.

"Ouch," Christoff replied in pain as I came crashing down against him.

With my hair still entangling his face, I moved my right arm towards his cell that lay in his left palm and grappled hold of it as I tried getting up. But he wasn't letting go of it without a fight.

"Not so easily Charloette," he said pulling me down by my wrist as I once again fell down.

"Curse you Christoff," I said animated before I confronted his face again.

For a moment our gazes interlocked.

"Let go," I said with a tremble in voice. But he gently shook his head making an enigmatic smile. I realized it was a "No"

At this my cheeks evidently got flustered before the train's whistle interrupted us back to reality.

He let go of my wrists as I took the cell and walked back onto the train.

There I sat by the window trying to find sense before Isen said to me

"Why don't you tell him?"

The very thought of an amatory relationship with that guy always makes me wanting to know his perception between friendship and love that bridges us both.

"Isen, it has to come from his side," I replied.

"He'll never say it even if he does. That's how he is,"

"I guess then, I'll just have to wait for the opportune time," I said ending the conversation.

It was one of the several videos stored in the data drive. One by one as I watched it all an unnerving feeling started welling up my heart, as I realised the bond we shared.

The final video was recorded by Newman Reeds. In it I realised the inspiration of Polaris came from me. He addressed me as her daughter before saying his final words,

"I know you blame me for everything that has happened to you in the past. Which is why I invented Polaris, to keep in touch with my daughter. The man I saw you with was the one I entrusted my life's work with. You are the dearest treasure I could ever have. This is my gift to you,"

With that the video ended as I kept staring at the monitor.

"Where does that lead us into?" Hosse asked me.

"Wherever Christoff is," I replied.

Phoenix Soul

"When two people love each other sincerely, then even the heavens would smile onto them. For those who love from their soul, write their own destiny,"

Such was our story that the stars aligned to change our fate.

Christoff was so intricately woven into everyone's life, that his absence after Angel Falls, left a huge void. I loved him more than I knew and he expressed it less than he did. Yet destiny wove us into one bond, and luckily we got engaged in the past.

Still wrestling with the guilt that made him leave me I drove through Springton Borough at night. Determined to make amends I reached towards Star-Crossed lake.

"That is where you'll find him," Isabell had said.

The place was lit by the innumerable stars that glistened against the red skyline. An expanse of heath covered countryside, lay covered in thawing snow-drops that trickled down the blades of grasses. Dandelion lined red roses enhanced its beauty while a small foot made path that led towards the glistening blue lake, lay amidst swirling, inviting you to join in, into the Spring that was waltzing in.

I stepped down the vehicle and walked down that path. Everywhere, I could hear birds singing a melody, emanating from the pink Bougainvillea trees that lay spangled everywhere. I had advanced quite a few distance when a music, so strikingly warm, so melodious, that it even made the trees flutter in its tune, erupted into my ears.

I started walking faster for I recognised the familiar tune. As I ran, the music got louder. My heart kept beating faster and finally there in front of the lakeside against the moon lit sky stood Christoff playing his violin.

The lake moved at its own pace and the birds sang. Amidst this, he was playing the Nightingale's melody.

The sync was so perfect, and yet so unnatural like fire and ice, that it forever left an impression upon me. Every chord of it expressed a feeling, and I could see Christoff completely engrossed.

I slowed down and came to a stop. Listening and feeling all his emotions that the tune conveyed. Even nature seemed entranced, for the radiance of the twinkling stars, had vanished under the cover of the swaying black clouds that were too heavy and could hold on no longer. And so rain drops started falling onto the warm earth gusting the air with grief.

Finally when he stopped, a loud silence fell over the vicinity. Everything ceased even time.

"Christoff," I called out to him.

The moment he heard my voice, his violin slithered away from his grasp. It fell down with a thump as he turned round and stood motionless looking in my direction.

The heavens knew the conflict in our hearts. For so long, Destiny had played her cards. But now nothing remained between us.

Only he and I stood . He held his emotions back. It was evident. And I could make him wait no longer.

I walked up to him in light steps and stood there facing him.

"I'm here....Christopher," I said at last.

"....Charloette.....what are you..."

"doing here," I said completing him.

"Ye..s," he said in a conflicted voice.

His behaviour seemed normal but his eyes gave it all away. He was crying inside. And I could see that even as we both were drenched wet in this cold rain.

"Why didn't you tell me the truth?" I asked.

"....I didn't want the guilt to burden you...And I still believe that you should leave... now.....It's the best choice for you,"

At this, my emotions overpowered me. I let go of all my anguish and raising my hand, I slapped him hard on the right.

This never hurt so badly. No, not the slap but his love.

The noise echoed in the stillness that was only broken by my sobbing and choking voice.

"You fool... don't you ever think of that again...." I said holding his face as I leaned towards him till our heads touched each other.

"You complete me Christoff, your love... makes my life worth living...," I said as tears trickled down from my eyes onto his face.

However he remained silent as his warm breath whisked past my cold face and I said it at last with a sad smile.

"Know what.... I may be the first person in the world to have ever slapped a guy and then tell him this...

I.... love you, Christoff. Always have and always will,"

Those 3 ever longing words finally evoked a response from him and wiping the tears of my face, he spoke in humble tones.

"Charl....don't love me so much..."

".....Can't help that," I cried out.

It was then, for the second time in life, did he caress my hair back onto my ear. Then, tilting his head forward, he finally kissed me on my lips.

So warm and loving was this stupid love, that even while it rained down, we stood there under the night sky...Nestled against each other's arms in embrace, never wanting to let go.

Epilogue

The music is being played as I walk down the aisle with Evelyn following me as my bridesmaid.

There on the altar Christoff stands awaiting me.

As I walk the red carpet, I see the familiar faces standing on the lawn. They all look at me and smile as I go past them.

I make my way up and there we two stand. The priest says his ritual and the time comes where we exchange our rings.

I first give him the ring, but he doesn't have one.

"You forgot the ring," I exclaim.

"No...no. Just wait a bit," he says.

Two minutes I stand there, when a car stops right in front. The Best Man steps down from the black car and walks towards us giving Christoff the ring.

"Here you go," he says handing him the ring.

"Thank God you made it here in time August," Christoff tells him.

August however, doesn't care about the delay. He simply keeps looking at Evelyn and smiles. When I look at my side, I realise that the reaction's mutual.

And so the ceremony takes place and The Padre finally says, "You may now kiss the bride,"

At this Christoff whispers something in his ear.

"Padre. May I," I say humbled.

"O! I forgot that. You may kiss the groom," he says turning towards me.

I give a smile and advance to kiss Christopher while the on-lookers simply laugh and cheer us on.

"You know they are laughing," I say to him.

"They are probably jealous," he says and we both share a kiss.

The wedding kicks off from then and everyone enjoy themselves out waltzing to their heart's rhythm.

No matter how much belittled one feels due to life's problems, our friends, our family, all our dear ones, they help us to get up. It's their love, that makes our not so perfect life, so goddamn beautiful.

And that's why this story isn't finished unless and until I narrate the fate of my beloved ones. Here I begin.

My friend, Alison found herself a life companion at our wedding. She and Adam are now happily married. They do make a lovely pair just like Isa and Hosse who are currently expecting their second child.

Speaking of couples.....August and Evelyn rekindled their romantic story. Those two are now dating each other.

Trisha finally succeeded in building her own hospital. This noble deed was made possible by my rum-pot buddy Isen's and Jeffrey's help.

You see, the Rum-Pot Inn, that Isabell gave to Isen after Hosse's return, got expanded by a little investment from Jeffrey into the world's most coveted food destination.

As for Charloette and me, we are more than happy looking after Jiva and Jaan, who is currently playing with Luce's puppies Lena, Lit and Pip.

Yes Luce did find a companion and is living with us in our new home back in Shaira. Finally... I'm sure... Grandma would be very happy watching over us and our little angels.

And so I bid adieu my friends, hoping you remember that

"There's a reason behind everything. And when you find it,

May spring waltz into your life as it did in ours."

www.ingramcontent.com/pod-product-compliance
Lightning Source LLC
LaVergne TN
LVHW041703070526
838199LV00045B/1178